ALICIA'S SECRET

Also by David Osborn

The Glass Tower

The French Decision

Love and Treason

Heads

Jessica and the Crocodile Knight *(children)*

Murder on Martha's Vineyard

Murder in the Napa Valley

Murder on the Chesapeake

The Last Pope

The Cape Cod Blue

A Cold Wind from the Andes

Looking Back: The Long Life of a Writer *(memoir)*

ALICIA'S SECRET

ALICIA'S SECRET

DAVID OSBORN

DAGMAR MIURA
LOS ANGELES

Published by Dagmar Miura
Los Angeles
www.dagmarmiura.com

Alicia's Secret

cover design by Jeremy Randolph

First published 2017

ISBN: 978-1-942267-35-5

for Robin, Raphaella, and Sebastian,
with love

CONTENTS

Matilda of Flanders

ONE

Ghosts. Have you ever seen one? I don't mean people pretending they are one, or thinking you see one when you're in a strange or scary house or walking past a graveyard, maybe. Or waking from deep sleep during the night and mistaking clothes draped over a chair for someone or something frighteningly alien. No, I mean an actual real "live" ghost. One that appears right in front of you, suddenly, and looks like any real person except you can see right through them, and while you are too terrified to breathe, almost, let alone scream, it calmly looks you up and down and says hello.

Well, that happened to me. Seriously, it *did*. And although I admit it happened in a country churchyard filled with old, old graves surrounding an ancient eleventh-century church in England, it was even more unexpected because it was a lovely summer morning with a warm and friendly sun filtering its golden light down through trees onto graying timeworn old tombstones and crosses. The sky was cloudless and blue; a little squirrel was hopping about searching out nuts it had buried; bees were buzzing around some wildflowers growing up against the old surrounding brick wall; somewhere a crow was calling; and from very high overhead there was the sound of a passing jetliner.

I'm Alicia, an American living in England, my high school years barely behind me and now studying at Oxford, of all places. Why England, and Oxford's famous hallowed halls? There are a number of reasons, but the real one, as you will see, began with my coming face-to-face with that ghost. That meeting in the churchyard, amidst its ancient gravestones and in broad sunny daylight, was the first in a series of events that changed everything about me, my whole life, and one I have always kept entirely to myself.

First of all, what was I doing in the churchyard, and for that matter, in England? Well, that summer, when I was still in school, my father, who writes, had to do some important research for a year at the British Library in London, and my older sister, Arielle, and I had to go with him. There were just the three of us because back in Connecticut, two years before, we had lost Mom and a little brother, Taylor (we always called him Tinker) in a car crash.

It was a terrible time. Poor Dad. Arielle who was very pretty (I'm not) and lives in a much different world from me with tons of friends, stopped seeing anyone for a long time, and for months I walked

around as though in a dream. I couldn't imagine anyone being dead, let alone Mom. And I missed Tinker so much.

I had always loved history, reading about times
and people who no longer existed, and my only sol-
ace was endlessly reading and reading mostly about
the lives of famous women in the past who might
have been dead, but were still with us in memory.
Somehow, that made me feel as though Mom was
still with us, too, because with me she had always
been famous herself.

Dad got worried about me, and stuck me for a
while with a psychiatrist, a Dr. Resus, who decided
that because I didn't have any friends and a big social
life, like Arielle did, that I was living in a fantasy world
and rejecting reality. I should be more outgoing, he
said, more sociable. He kept citing Arielle as an example. But I'm *not* Arielle. I adore her, but I never cared
about iPods and iPads and cell phones and Facebook
and texting and all that, and I was even less interested
in painting my fingernails and toes and who the latest
rock star was and gossiping endlessly with other girls.
At school I was seen as *different,* and a lot of people
avoided me like the plague just because I liked mostly
to be alone and to read and sketch things I saw that
interested me as unusual. When Mom left us I was
learning to play the cello, too. I stopped practicing,
though, because Arielle couldn't bear the mournful
sound it made. She said it was like Mom and Tinker's
funerals all over again.

In England, we were allowed to take a year off

from school and, since we'd lived in the country in Connecticut, Dad arranged a home for us about a mile from Henley, a historic town right on the Thames River in the Thames Valley west of London, which is mostly fields and farms and small towns and, of course, Oxford. Halfway between the big, old yellow-brick country house we rented and Henley is the churchyard I was in. The church itself goes back to ten hundred and something and is half covered with Ivy and has a big rusty clock face in its square-topped tower that looks down on all the ancient graves, where the writing on crosses and headstones is weathered almost unrecognizable.

We both had time on our hands, and with Dad deep in his work that particular day, Arielle had gone up to London shopping with a new friend she'd made, who lives in a big house with dogs and horses, directly across the Thames river from us. I biked into Henley to do some reading in the library there—it has a great history section—and pick up a new sketch pad at the art shop. Coming back, I decided to go into the churchyard and sketch some of the gravestones. They never spooked me the way they did Arielle. To me they always looked friendly, and I didn't think of the people buried there as skeletons or even just earth. I thought of them as people like Mom and Tinker. Names on gravestones don't tell you much about them, and I could never stop wondering who they had been and what their lives had been like. Were they rich or poor, famous or just ordinary like me? Graveyards must all have a bit of everything. Just like life.

I parked my bike up against the mossy old brick wall which went around the whole churchyard, pushed open the creaky wooden gate, and went in. There was nobody there, only the little squirrel hopping about, some sparrows up under the eaves of the church itself, and an old man in workman's clothes. When he saw me, he tipped his cap and said, "Mornin', Miss. I'm Henry. Just tidying. Can I help?" When I told him I was there to sketch, he nodded and said, "Make yourself at home, miss," and went on working.

It had rained the day before, the grass was still wet. I got out my pad and a pencil from my waist bag and plunked down on a gravestone that had fallen and dried and began to sketch some roses climbing up part of the brick wall, and some wildflowers being hummed about by bees.

I'd been sketching away a while, and the old workman had left, when it suddenly began. By "it" I mean this crazy thing that in a way changed my whole life. I began to get the oddest feeling about the particular person who lay beneath the gravestone I was sitting on. It's hard to explain because there didn't seem any reason for it. I felt like whoever had been buried there long ago was … well, someone like me. I told myself that was silly and to stop imagining things.

But the feeling kept coming back to me as I sketched. It was as though she—I was *sure* it was a she—knew I was there and wanted to tell me something. It was downright eerie; I'd never felt anything like it, not ever. I kept pushing it out of my head, but when I'd become tired of sketching and realized it was time to go home, the feeling came back stronger than ever, that someone down there was reaching up to me. On some sort of nutty impulse, I went and picked a little bunch of the wildflowers and laid them on the gravestone. "Here," I said. "These are for you."

Then the moment passed, and feeling myself again, except a little foolish, I collected my things and headed out. Who on earth leaves flowers on the grave of someone who's been dead for maybe hundreds of years when you don't even know who they were? I was on the flagstone path that went from the church door to the rickety wooden gate in the brick wall when I heard the voice.

"Please don't go. Please."

It gave me quite a jolt because I'd been sitting there all this time thinking I was alone after Henry, the old workman, left. I looked around and saw no one. Okay, it had to be someone in the church. But I saw no open windows or doors. So maybe seated and hidden by a tall gravestone?

The voice again. "We can talk if you'd like."

I really chilled then and somehow found my own voice. "Who—who said that?"

"I did. And it was so lovely of you to put flowers on my grave. Thank you."

I can't remember how I felt or thought after that. I went into store dummy mode, and my brain froze solid. And then I saw her. She was my age, with blue, blue eyes and hair the color of straw that seemed to grow in every direction and have been hacked short here and there, helter-skelter. She was wearing funny-looking almost canvas pants and beat-up leather boots and a long, rough-looking tunic made out of something like burlap that was tied around her waist with a bit of old rope. She was seated on the fallen gravestone I'd been sitting on, her arms hugging her knees, and she wore a smile that looked as though it would burst into light laughter any second.

Have you ever, ever had every part of you suddenly go on strike: arms, legs, everything …? I tried to move, I couldn't. I wanted to believe anything except where I was and what was happening. This wasn't someone pretending to be a ghost. I was looking right through her at gravestones and crosses. One terrifying thought seemed to possess my entire body—*this is a ghost—for real.*

TWO

*T*he ghost's smile faded. "Oh, dear. I see I've badly frightened you. I'm sorry. Please don't be afraid. I couldn't possibly hurt you even if I wanted to. Which I certainly don't. I'm Elvira, and you were right to think I wasn't old. But tell me who you are. What's your name, and what are you doing here?"

She waited. I slowly came back to life. Sort of. I was in the old Norman churchyard with its worn gravestones and crosses and grassy lawn and the mossy old surrounding brick wall. I'd gone to get wildflowers to put on the gravestone that had fallen over. It was awfully quiet. The only sound I heard was the bees after the wildflowers.

And I was staring at a ghost. A real one. Worse, I was all alone with her, and all my warm thoughts about people buried in churchyards evaporated. No matter what she said, she might suddenly drag me deep down under the gravestone she was sitting on where there had to be some kind of terrible evil. I tried not to picture moldy old bones and rotting coffins.

Then I heard someone speaking and realized it was me. "I—I'm Alicia," my voice said. "I live up the lane a ways." I pointed in its direction and wished I was there.

"I know. In the big yellow brick house with the garden and swimming pool. It looks down over pastures at the Thames. Lucky you."

That flummoxed me. How did she know that? I managed a few more words. The ghost, who said she was Elvira, laughed.

"I'm glad you came today. It's been ever so long since I talked to a living person. Four hundred years, actually."

Four hundred years? I fused out all over again. But I didn't get a chance to think further because right before my eyes the ghost called Elvira simply vanished. I mean one second she was there, and the next she wasn't.

Before I had any chance to wonder, I heard the creaky sound of the rickety gate in the brick wall. It was the vicar.

He saw me and said politely, "Hello, there, young lady. Came to sketch, did you?" A gentle smile broke his white-bearded face. He was bent with age, and his voice quavered. "How nice, how nice. Lovely day for sketching." He waved his cane at the church. "If you want anything, I'll be in the vestry."

You know what it is to feel relieved—like one thousand percent plus, maybe? Here was sudden safety. If I rushed to him, he'd be able to protect me if the ghost came back and decided to do something awful. But I didn't. One half of me said I didn't want to seem like I couldn't handle a ghost; the other half said if the ghost didn't come back, he'd think I was a serious candidate for the state hospital.

He went on with the hesitant steps of old age. I watched him enter the church. The door looked as old as the rest of it and had huge bolts and iron straps holding it together, and rusty iron hinges and a lock that looked like it needed a key as big as a canoe paddle.

It had hardly closed behind him when I heard Elvira saying, "Such a nice old man. He and old Henry who keeps us all tidy. We've had some mean ones occasionally over the years, bothering around our church and churchyard. They've been quite annoying sometimes. The worst though are the tour buses that come because we are so historic." Her laughter burst out again, mischievously. "The last time one came, I managed to frighten one woman half to death. I made her think the place was haunted."

Just like that, she was back, seated again on the old gravestone, her arms hugging her knees and looking pleased at having frightened somebody.

Brain dead here managed to blurt out the obvious. "You disappeared."

"Of course. We only come out to be seen by people we want to see us."

I'd got some of my shattered nerves together when I decided not to rush for help to the vicar. I started to tell her I thought ghosts only appeared on Halloween but stopped short of the word *ghost* because I thought she might be insulted and get angry, and then what? Who knew what her unfriendly side might be like?

Elvira read my mind. "Hey, say 'ghost.' I don't care. After all, that's what I am, right? And you thought ghosts only appeared on Halloween? Never. Not me, anyway. I wouldn't demean myself so. Halloween's for the spirits of murderers and thieves and other wicked people."

To my surprise, I began not to feel frightened of her. Curiosity took over. I wanted to know why Elvira had died so young, and asked her.

"I was carried away by the plague," she answered.

The plague? That chilled me all over again. I'd read about the plague—almost everyone has. It was centuries ago and killed nearly half the people in Europe.

Again it was as though she could read minds. "Hold on. You're thinking of the great plague in 1350." She laughed. "Good heavens, I'm not that old. The plague that got me was a small English one in 1588. We used to call it the 'sweats.' Took you off in twenty-four hours."

Nudged again and then some; 1588 somehow made the four-hundred years more real.

I found myself staring at her and seeing nothing else. Not the churchyard or the church, not even the little squirrel who had hopped close between us.

He wasn't scared of ghosts, that's for sure. I could see only Elvira, her crazy, messed-up haircut that looked like someone had run amok with a scythe in a wheat field, her mischievous smile, the blue, blue eyes. I tried to sort things out. I tried to see Elvira back in Shakespeare's day and couldn't. I couldn't imagine her being anywhere at any time except right now in the churchyard. She was that *alive.*

"1588? But that was when Elizabeth the First was queen." I thought I ought to let Elvira know I wasn't a total dummy and added, "She was England's greatest queen."

Elvira jumped on that one. "Elizabeth? That old misery? Nonsense."

I retreated. "Well, who was then?"

"Matilda of Flanders, of course. Everyone knows that."

Elvira's lighthearted smile had disappeared. I had visions again of moldy bones and rotting coffins down deep somewhere. I quickly retreated and asked Elvira where she lived—that's to say, when she was alive.

Her smile came back. "Not far. My father had a farm down river past the Old Plough Horse. That's that old pub a half mile beyond you. He had a proper manor with barns and stables and everything, and big fancy stone posts holding up the front gate with his name, Thomas Brown, on them. Like some fancy gentleman. And a mean old devil he was, too."

The anger in her voice surprised me, and I tried to think of something harmless to say. "Did you ever go up to London?"

Laughter rippled out. "London town? Almost never. I was strictly a country girl."

The way she said it, I immediately imagined her running barefoot through spring pastures dotted with wildflowers or raking hay in a freshly mowed field under a hot sun. "Did you have a boyfriend?"

"No. But I was betrothed. The plague got me the day before my wedding."

With that one, another jolt. "You were getting *married?*"

"Yes, and he was a good enough lad, too, I suppose, and it was either marry him or face another year of beatings from my Dad. After I'd gone, he went and married a horror, the silly boy."

"But, but …" Thinking how could anyone get married so young.

"I know," she said. "I was past marrying age, but nobody had wanted me until then."

That did it. I couldn't add it up. My age and marriage? I tried to see myself in a wedding gown and walking up the aisle. No way.

"Wasn't I lucky?" Elvira said. "Another year or so, and nobody would have wanted me."

Lucky? That was sick. What she said meant that if I had lived when she did, I could have found myself pushed up the aisle and then have some horrid pimply boy all over me. Thanks. No wonder Shakespeare wrote so many tragedies. Thinking that, a light bulb suddenly went on.

"Elvira," I said. "If you lived that long ago, how come you talk the way you do? I mean, back then, didn't everyone speak differently? My sister had to read somebody called Chaucer in school, and I can't get onto that scene, no matter what."

"You're right," Elvira replied. "But I don't speak to you at all, Alicia. I'm just sending you my thoughts, and you are putting them into your language yourself."

I didn't quite see how that was possible, but I didn't want to rain on my welcome by bugging her about it. I changed course. We'd left the great queen business hanging in the wind, so I charged up my nerve and asked what and where Flanders was, which is where she said the queen named Matilda came from. It didn't sound English to me. Not even Shakespearean.

Elvira didn't seem in the least annoyed at the question. "Flanders," she explained, "was what is now Belgium, along with a good piece of Holland and a slice of northeastern France. But it wasn't a country the way you think of one now. There were no nations back then. Just kingdoms and so forth. Land and people were the personal property of barons or counts or kings."

I tried to picture it. Holland and Belgium are flat and have a lot of canals. It must have been pretty much the same back then "Okay," I said, "but how did she get to be an English queen?"

"By marrying William the Conqueror. You must have heard of him."

I told her I had, and about how he crossed the Channel and defeated the English. I'd once learned in school how that meant the Norman language, which was French, and Norman-style government based on Roman law instead of Germanic tribal rule, which caused England to become what it is today, and because of that, America, too.

"Right," Elvira said. "And if it hadn't been for Matilda, William's Conquest would have failed. Guaranteed."

"Really? Why? And if she was first from Flanders and then a Norman, how could she be an *English* queen?"

Elvira didn't answer. Instead she gave me a long strange look and then said. "Alicia, you're very lonely, aren't you?"

It caught me completely off guard. "I—I'm not," I stammered.

"Yes, you are. And especially so ever since your mum died. Your sister and you are miles apart, and you really don't have any of your own. Friends, I mean. Not ones you could feel safe with. Arielle's the family 'movie star' and always makes you feel like an ugly duckling who has no chance ever to be a swan. You're mostly hiding in a world of your own, which is history and which is very real to you, and not just dry reading in books. And otherwise you're into art and music and not into all the stuff everyone else is—computer games and pods and pads and cells and selfies, all that—and so you feel forever left out. Look at you today. You came here all alone, didn't you? To the churchyard filled with ghosts like me."

She rippled with light laughter at that. And I couldn't help smiling back. She was right about everything. I was lonely. I felt awkward and out of place with other people and at times thoroughly worthless, especially when Dad got angry with me because I couldn't figure out things on the laptop he insisted I use.

"Tell you what," Elvira said. "How would you like to meet some of my friends? They're much more your kind. One is an artist and they all love music. Oh, I don't mean the current pop stuff. One's into Gregorian chants—what the monks used to sing in the Middle Ages, and another's into Renaissance music like Vivaldi, strings and mandolins and all that. And one actually knew Bach. They're ghosts like me, of course, but that shouldn't bother you, and I'm sure they'd love to meet you."

That made my head spin. None of it made even zero sense. Elvira, who had died more than four hundred years ago, was calmly sitting on her fallen gravestone as though there was nothing unusual in her being here. Knowing all about the secret me and talking about my meeting other ghosts. If I'd been on ecstasy or acid or some other stupid drug, I could have chalked it all up to hallucination. But I wasn't. I looked around. All those silent gravestones and the brick wall, the old Norman church with its bell tower and rusty clock face, the towering trees, the soft grass half-covered with autumn leaves, the little squirrel hopping about, the vicar coming by.

No, it was real. And so was Elvira. I shook myself. My mind said *Don't just sit there staring like the village idiot.* Say something. *I* didn't get the chance to. The church bell suddenly sounded the hour, and almost at the same moment a door creaked open, and the vicar came out of the church, locking the door behind him.

"Ah, still here Miss, are you? It's my lunchtime. Perhaps yours, too. But stay as long as you like." He went slowly on his way, his cane leaving small prodding marks in the turf by the flagstones to the gate.

Of Elvira, there wasn't a sign. There was just her voice coming from somewhere around the fallen gravestone.

"I'd love it if you came again," the voice said.

I left the churchyard.

THREE

I didn't sleep much that night, and the next day I felt completely disconnected. I'd never felt like that before; there'd always been a connection to someone or something or an anchor of some kind to reality. Now, it was as if I'd suddenly found myself on the moon. Half of me said play it safe, don't go back to the churchyard, reconnect with the familiar and easy, with what Dr. Resus called "now"; the other half felt drawn to it as though by a magnet.

The other half won. It was like a magnet was pulling me, and I finally got my act together, but just the same it took a couple of days before I found an excuse to go biking by myself, even though it was cloudy and cool and looked like I might get rained on. I hadn't got halfway there, though, when fresh doubts surged. It might all be a trap. The ground around the graves might suddenly open up and I'd find myself falling into something too horrible to even think of. And had I actually met a ghost? A real live one? Maybe when I sat down on the old fallen gravestone I'd fallen dead asleep and dreamed it. My mind went round and around until, by the time I reached the old Norman church, I was convinced that Elvira, with her short corn-colored hair and blue, blue eyes, had been a fantasy trip.

Just the same, I leaned my bike against the mossy brick wall and went slowly through the rickety old gate and then to the fallen gravestone. "Elvira?" I could barely say the name without feeling like the original village idiot because I had convinced myself that there wouldn't be a response.

"Elvira? It's me. Alicia."

When there was still no answer, I gave up. I was right. What on earth was I doing there? If I actually *had* seen a ghost, what made me think I would see it a second time?

I turned away from the fallen gravestone, That's when I heard the familiar laughter rippling lightly through the cold air. "Hello. What took you so long?" And there she was, seated on the fallen gravestone just as she had been the day before with a slightly teasing smile and as though rain meant nothing to her.

Seeing her actually *there,* I nearly keeled over with relief.

There was a gust of wind and a first few drops of the threatened rain. she saw me wince at it and laughed. "We don't get wet," she said. "Or hot. But you do, and you'd be better off inside."

"Where?"

"The church, silly. Come on."

I followed her to the door, protesting that it was locked. "The vicar never leaves it open," I said.

"Maybe it's locked for *you*," Elvira laughed. And with that, she simply walked through it. One moment she was on my side of the door, and the next, I heard it being unlocked from the inside, and it opened, and there she was. She took in my look and laughed again. "I'm a ghost, remember?"

Without another word, she headed for the front pew by the choir seats and waved to me to follow, and we went up the center aisle, the big stone paving blocks of which were almost worn into a ditch from generations of people's feet. Light, filtering through some lovely stained-glass windows, sent a shaft of pale yellow and red onto the tombs of two knights buried under the floor at a place surrounded by an iron railing. Wide dark shadows from the huge hand-hewn beams holding up the roof were stretched almost like menacing barriers the width of the rows of creaky wooden pews, which were all shiny from people sitting on them for hundreds of years.

Elvira stood staring up at the ancient organ. "When the sexton plays it," she said, "it squeaks like a thousand mice had found homes in its pipes." She laughed. "And maybe they have." She plunked down on the altar floor, and I sank onto a front-row pew facing her. "You don't have to worry about the dear old vicar today," she said. "He's got a cold and is resting in bed. Now. Friends. Which would you like to meet first? Matilda, Sofonisba, or Lucie? I think maybe Matilda."

That shook me. Matilda? Could she possibly mean the one she said was England's greatest queen?

She read my mind and said, "Yes, I mean Queen Matilda. We talked about her when we first met."

I laughed in spite of myself. I thought she was having me on. "Oh, come on! Why would any queen ever want to meet me?"

Elvira's eyes widened in mock surprise. "You think that? Really? Well, why don't you ask her?"

"Sure, sure. And just how do I do that?"

"It's easy. You turn around."

I saw Elvira looking behind me and turned to see a woman Mom's age, when she lived, standing close by in the aisle. It gave me a real voltage shot because when we'd come in, there wasn't anyone in the church except Elvira and me. Like Elvira, she had a strange, gauzy quality, and I realized I could see right through her, so for a moment I went into the same state I had when I first met Elvira. Everything in me sort of went like a blizzard whiteout.

She was not much taller than me, and slender, and her hair was beginning to show signs of gray. In a soft voice, she said "Hello, Alicia. I'm Matilda."

I just stared. I couldn't speak. I knew this must really be Queen Matilda. But was it? Was it someone pretending to be, and Elvira playing tricks on me? She didn't look like a queen; she looked like a perfectly normal person. She was wearing a plain long colorless dress with a shawl thrown over her head and looped around her neck and soft ankle-high slippers with pointed toes. She spoke again, and I can't remember what she said. I can only remember there was something about her that said "authority," but that there was warmth and kindness, too.

I finally came to my senses when she said, "Elvira's told me all about you. Did you think I wouldn't come?"

I began to unfreeze when she smiled and seemed to understand the shock she'd given me.

"And please, you mustn't be uncomfortable just because I was a queen. That was a very long time ago, and it doesn't make me especially important now. So you don't have to curtsey or anything silly like that. Or call me 'your majesty' the way Elvira does when she's teasing me. Just Matilda will do."

She came and settled herself comfortably on the altar steps, where Elvira joined her. "Do sit down, my dear," she told me.

I was still standing like a dummy, and that brought me to my senses. A queen commands and you obey. I collapsed back down into the pew. Queen Matilda smiled and continued.

"That's better," and then, "Elvira tells me you'd like to know how I got to be an English queen and what I did to help my husband with the *Conquest*."

I found my voice. "Oh, yes." And, in spite of myself, I added, "ma'am."

"And better you hear it from me than William, I think, don't you Elvira? William could be quite alarming, you know. He was, after all, first and foremost a warrior. In spite of his becoming King of England and ruling wisely, I still often see him in my mind as coming to me, fresh from battle, his armor covered in blood and his sword still unsheathed."

As I was conjuring up a ghastly picture of a ferocious knight who reveled in killing, I heard the ghostly queen say, "But enough of William for the moment. There was a lot in my life besides that sort of thing, as well as long before him."

"Like all the growing-up years when you were a princess," Elvira said.

"That first, then," Matilda agreed, and she started right off. "I was born in 1031, Alicia, and I'm sure you know that Europe was a very different place then than it is today. Most of Spain was part of a vast Arab empire that stretched all across North Africa. France was made up of independent dukedoms more or less ruled by a king whose only power was that he'd been anointed by the pope."

"That meant he was chosen by God, so nobody dared challenge him," Elvira said.

"That's right," Matilda agreed, and continued. "Germany was a federation of states ruled by an elected emperor and, like most of Eastern Europe, was still pagan. Europe had gone a long way downhill from Rome's collapse when Roman law and order was abandoned along with Roman towns and cities and roads. Most of Europe had gone back to forest roamed by robbers and wolves and ruled by lawless barons. People called it the *Dark Ages*.

"And so I came into a world, Alicia, when Europe was a dangerous place. You took your life in your hands if you went from one town to another without an armed escort. Any time I left our castle, my father had me surrounded by a dozen heavily armed knights along with a score of foot soldiers."

"But that was mostly because you were a princess," Elvira said.

"Well, yes, perhaps," Matilda admitted. "Ordinary people were far more at risk, poor devils. They were the first victims of any war. Victors in battle would burn villages and crops and steal cattle and sheep and goats and any poor woman they could lay hands on. Every road they traveled would soon be littered with corpses, and clouds of smoke would hang over every village and field."

It was just at that point that I realized I'd virtually stopped thinking of Elvira or Queen Matilda as ghosts, and especially not ghosts from hundreds of years in the past. Sitting close together on the altar steps and looking back at me from just a few feet away, they were more like warm and friendly people I could have chanced to meet anywhere. I remembered Elvira telling me where Flanders was, and I got up my nerve and asked if Flanders was part of the German Federation.

"Yes. It was, although reluctantly."

"Then was it pagan?"

Matilda smiled. "No, we in Flanders were Christian. That along with our flax and wool and weaving industries made us the federation's most powerful and wealthiest state. Our town of Bruges was the most important port on Europe's north coast. We were way ahead, also, in music, art, and architecture, and that included the French and Italians."

Somehow that made it easier for me to ask another question. "What sort of government did you have?"

"My father, Count Baldwin the Second, *was* the government. Under him we had a system called feudalism."

I had always pictured feudalism as a dark and foreboding dictatorship. "Wasn't that bad?"

"It was right for the times. Don't forget that except for a handful of monks in far-flung monasteries and a few nobility, higher churchmen, and kings, nobody could read or write, so people were incapable of governing themselves. And they needed protection. That came from the knight on whose land the peasant lived and for which he provided work or produce and often soldiering. The knight, in turn, would contribute produce and soldiers to the baron who had granted him the land just as the baron provided the same to his ruling count or duke.

"One of my earliest memories—I guess I was four or five—was the main hall of our castle, which had been all decorated with banners. Father was seated on a big oaken chair placed where he normally sat at the long table we ate on in a part of the great hall that was raised a step or two. It was the castle's largest room. Standing to each side of him were all his barons and leading knights, each holding his shield bearing his coat of arms. Clustered at one end of the room were all the barons' and knights' ladies. At the other end, stood the *steward,* who ran the castle and most of my father's affairs along with the various captains of the men-at-arms who stood at rigid attention in their chain mail and steel and leather helmets while holding their long spears erect. My mother had brought me to watch as a once rebellious baron knelt in the reeds and rushes that covered the stone or dirt floor and handed his sword to my father and swore allegiance to him.

"It was terribly smoky. There weren't any chimneys in those days, just a hole in the roof for the smoke to escape through, and most of it didn't. The great hall was almost the only part of the castle that was heated except for iron braziers filled with red-hot coals in my room and my parents' rooms. In the middle of it, there was an open fire on a circle of flat stones. Otherwise, it was cold everywhere. Cold and dark. A castle really only sheltered you from rain, snow, and wind. Inside the temperature was just like outside.

"I remember, too, when I was a little girl at mass in the chapel in the winter. The floor was packed earth until my father paved it later with stone. We didn't have window glass then, and snow would blow through the narrow openings that archers shot through if we were attacked and which served as windows. Mass took well over an hour. Kneeling until my knees ached and my teeth chattered, I thought I'd die right there."

As she spoke, I tried to imagine it—a snowy

wind blowing down on a half frozen child. I almost couldn't.

"It was always dark, too, until the sun rose," she went on to say. "If you were nobility or rich, as I fortunately was, there were candles and crude oil lamps, little clay dishes filled with burning animal fat. There were also resin torches made from sticks dipped in tree sap. They were usually fitted into iron wall brackets, although you could carry them, too, to light your way."

"What if you *weren't* nobility or rich?" I asked.

"The merchants and the better-off townspeople had much of what we had. The peasantry out in the country, which was most people because our towns were very small, usually had no light except from the open fires they cooked on. There were no such things as stoves. They rose at the first glimmer of dawn and went to bed at sunset. Except for eating or repairing tools, there wasn't anything else to do. They couldn't read, remember? And even if they'd been able to, printing hadn't been invented yet. Books were all handwritten, and just one was worth more than a whole year's earnings for a peasant."

"What were the books all about?"

"Books? Oh, nothing like yours today. The few that existed were all religious texts by church philosophers and the poetry and thoughts of Greeks and Romans who had been dead for a thousand years or more. Everything back then, Alicia, was God. God and the Church. I had to attend mass twice a day. And vespers at night and first prayers at three in the morning."

"As a child?"

"My whole life."

"But that's awful."

"It didn't seem so back then. In all of Europe until only a few hundred years ago, people had nothing in their lives to believe in and trust except God and the Holy family—Christ and the blessed Virgin Mother and the saints. They were reality and gave them strength to keep going."

"They and superstition," Elvira said.

"And superstition indeed," Matilda agreed. "The devil and his workers were absolutely real. Witches and ghouls and hobgoblins were everywhere, and there were all sorts of terrible beliefs. My father had one of his cooks flogged senseless because he caught the man stirring the soup counterclockwise, and that could bring the devil's curse on the whole family."

"But that's crazy," I exclaimed.

"Oh, there was even worse. Women who shied from mass were often labeled witches and burned or drowned for their pains. If someone's child didn't seem like other children, there'd be fear it was a *changeling*. That was a fairy who had stolen the soul of the real child and replaced it with its own. People would put a shoe in a bowl of soup or try to bake a loaf of bread in an egg shell, and if the baby laughed, they'd know it was a fairy and hold it over a fire to chase the fairy out of it."

As I tried to make sense of that horror and wondered how many poor children had died because of it, Matilda said, "You're shocked, I know. How terribly cruel. And worse, how awfully ignorant and stupid. But unfortunately, that's just the way things were. Total obedience to God on one hand, superstition on the other. You prayed endlessly, or you'd risk being taken away by witches or ghouls."

The words were hardly out of her mouth when she and Elvira simply disappeared as though they had never been there at all, just the way Elvira had when I first met her. One second their gauzy figures were seated side by side on the steps up to the altar, Matilda more serious and every inch a queen, Elvira always ready, whenever possible, to make light of things. The next, I found myself alone.

But not for long. There was the sound of the big church door creaking and rumbling open, and I heard a man say commandingly, "This way, ladies."

I turned to see a balding, ruddy-faced person in khaki trousers and a striped red and white blazer entering the church. He was followed by a small crowd of women, mostly older, voicing their appreciation for everything in sight.

"The church you are entering, ladies," the man said, "is one of the earliest examples we have of Norman architecture. It was built, we believe, shortly after the Conquest, probably about the year 1075. The writing on a stone plaque set into the wall here by the baptistery still bears the name of Queen Matilda, who ordered its construction. She was the wife of William the Conqueror and England's first actual reigning queen."

There were oohs and aahs about everything, and I

found myself almost giggling. If they only knew that the queen herself had been there sitting on the steps to the altar just seconds before they came in.

FOUR

efore I had even met Matilda, I had made
up my mind that if I so much as hinted
I'd been talking to real live ghosts, I'd be
an instant candidate for some creepy old English
shrink insisting I tell him what drugs I was on. And
Arielle would have told all her new English friends
as well as all the ones back in the States she texted to
every day, news that she had a crazy sister.

Elvira, and now Matilda, would have to remain
my secret from everyone. And forever.

Just the same, I nearly blew it. That night at dinner, Dad suddenly turned to me and asked "How are
you making out with the iPad?" He'd given me one
just before we'd all come over to England.

"Okay." It must have sounded terribly ungrateful,
but I couldn't think of what else to say, because right
from the beginning, how to make it work defied me.

That would have been the end of it except Arielle had to come on with, "Okay, meaning she almost never uses it. I wish you'd given it to me."

Arielle and I get along well, but occasionally we bristle a little at each other.

"I do, too use it," I said.

"Sure. Once a year."

It was too late. She'd got me going. "There are lots of people like me, Arielle," I said, "who don't sit all day on their cell phones or iPads."

"Oh? Like who?"

And I completely forgot myself. "Like Elvira," I said. "She's never even seen an iPad."

Ariel's eyes widened. "And who, pray, is Elvira?"

I came to my senses and tried to retreat. "Never mind."

"Which means you're making her up."

Dad sought peace. "Elvira. What a lovely name. Where did you meet her?"

I desperately remembered the nearby lock at the Thames River. "At the lock. Watching them lower a boat."

"How nice you met someone," Dad said. "Bring her home, if you like."

"Okay," I said, knowing how impossible that would be.

Getting into bed a while later, I swore I'd never again let my guard down.

I was dying to hear more of how Matilda lived,

but it was the next afternoon before I could get to the churchyard, and when I called Elvira there was no answer. My heart sank. Perhaps she and Matilda had decided not to come again. But then, thinking she might be inside and have forgotten, I went to the church door. It was locked. I knocked and called softly, and the creepiest thing happened. The door slowly swung open all by itself. It scared me silly until I heard a light ripple of laughter and knew that Elvira, at least, was there. What a relief. I made my way up the darkened aisle, and sure enough there she was, and Matilda with her, both seated on the steps to the altar.

"Scared you," Elvira said.

"Stop it," Matilda scolded.

But Elvira couldn't. When I told them about my close call, she went off into gales of laughter. Matilda was less amused. "Sounds like my sister and me."

"You had a sister?"

"Indeed, and two brothers. We were as close as kittens but had fights just the same. But dear Alicia, do be more careful. Nobody will ever believe you if you bumble again. They'll start thinking something is seriously wrong with you, and you don't want that."

I promised. You can bet I did.

"Now, where was I?" Matilda asked.

Yanking my head back into the eleventh century, I said, "You were saying how smoky the big hall was because you didn't have chimneys, just a hole in the roof. What was the rest of your castle like?"

"Not at all what I'm sure you imagine. It was made

of wood. Stone castles in northern Europe hadn't been invented yet. And our castles were far smaller than the ones you see in pictures, which mostly began to be built a hundred years after me. My father's was on a low hill and only two stories high. It was attached to the inside of a high wooden wall manned by archers and soldiers. The wall surrounded a large, open space we called a *bailey* where there were gardens and stables for the horses. In the middle of ours was a tall wooden tower called the *donjon,* a heavily fortified place to retreat to if the walls were breeched by an enemy and the castle burned down. It always had a well in it for water.

"I thought a donjon was a deep underground place where prisoners were kept," I said.

"You're thinking of a dungeon. A donjon is spelled differently, even though it sounds the same."

Elvira laughed. "One was up, the other down, and half the time you never left either alive."

"Unfortunately true," Matilda said.

"What was your castle like? I mean to live in," I asked.

"Well, as I told you before, even among the nobility there was no heat and very little light. There were no windows; just the archers' narrow slits, and there was also no running water or sanitation as you know it, although most of the nobility were clean personally. Everyone in my court bathed at least once a week."

"But what about everyone else? I mean people who didn't live in castles."

"The peasantry in the fields, the townspeople? They rarely bathed, if ever, except in the summer, and in streams or rivers. How could they?"

I asked Matilda how she managed to bathe without running water.

"Servants would bring boiling water up to my room in buckets and pour it into a big wooden tub for me."

"Did you have many servants?"

"In the castle, probably over a hundred. I only had five personal ones. And, of course, there were my several ladies-in-waiting, and I could call on any of the household servants if I needed them."

"Just when you were a princess?"

"Yes, all during my childhood."

A hundred servants?! Out of sight, I thought. But thinking even a thousand servants couldn't have helped much while getting undressed to bathe in the dead of winter with ice and snow coming right through the window. I said, "But what about heat?"

Matilda smiled at my reaction. "Oh, in my bedroom, anyway, there was an iron brazier always kept filled with red-hot coals brought up from the kitchen. And in the main hall there was always the open log fire on a raised stone part of the floor. In the winter it was kept ablaze night and day. You just had to be careful where you walked because occasionally a red-hot coal would jump out and land right where you were going to plant a foot."

"Ouch!" I said, making Matilda laugh.

"That was your room and your castle," Elvira said.

"And you were a princess. The rest of the world ..."
She shrugged pointedly.

"I know. Half the time they froze," Matilda agreed. She sighed. "Sometimes knowing that spoiled my being kept warm the way I was. In the winter, when I got older, and I'd ride out on my *palfrey* with some of my ladies, the women coming out to see me were usually shivering and blue from the cold. And the children often didn't have shoes with their poor little feet freezing in the snow and mud. I remember one especially awful day. There was a north wind, and it had rained. The roads close around our castle were frozen ruts. I had four ladies-in-waiting with me and a page boy and a half-dozen mounted men-at-arms as guards.

"We passed a little group of women with five children. The women had wrapped rags around the children's feet, and one woman had taken off her coat and put it around two children and stood in nothing herself but a tattered chemise that didn't cover half her nakedness. I stopped my party and ordered each of my ladies-in-waiting to take a child up on her saddle and wrap her coat around it. I did the same, and I told the mothers to get up on the horses with the men-at-arms. One of my ladies was shocked and tried to refuse, but I was a princess, and my word was law where everyone except my father was concerned. I turned my whole party back to the castle and ordered the mothers and children to be dropped off at the kitchen and fed and clothed properly before they were sent home.

"When my father heard, he scolded me. He said, 'Now every peasant will be out on the roadside wanting refuge in our kitchens.'

"It was the first time I had ever stood up to my father. I said to him, 'Well, then, my Lord, you had better enlarge your kitchens.' As I stormed off, I saw my father hiding a smile. He was a good and kind man.

"Life for the poor back then was dawn to dusk utter misery." She shook her head, trying to rid herself of the memory, and added quickly, "But there are happier things to talk about."

I wondered how anybody could study in cold like that, so I asked how they heated their schools.

"Schools? There weren't any. And of course no radio or television. And there were no doctors or medicine, either. Old age was thirty, if you weren't killed long before that by disease or in wars or by bandits."

"Or burned at the stake or hung or beheaded for some supposed crime or sin," Elvira added. "Half the time they didn't bother to lock people up, they just got rid of them. Things weren't much better in my day, either. You were hung for stealing a loaf of bread. Or tied to a stake with wood piled around and burned to death because you saw God differently than the king or queen."

I couldn't imagine not having any medicine or food or living all winter with no heat. "I don't see how anyone managed to live," I said.

"A lot of them didn't," Matilda replied sadly. "Only two out of every three children born reached the age of five." She added quickly, "But I don't mean to make it seem too awful. And fortunately my life wasn't. We didn't have any of your modern conveniences, but we had a very cultivated way of life. Among the nobility we wrote poetry and philosophy and composed music. I was raised to speak French and Greek and especially Latin, which was what everything was written in. Most of the nobility spoke to each other in Latin. We had very strict rules about manners, too. Except in the most intimate circumstances, we always spoke to each other quite formally. We had magnificent churches and chapels and some wonderful artwork and wore lovely clothes, silks, and furs; all noblewomen had beautiful jewelry—the same as you have today: diamonds and sapphires and emeralds and even pearls, which came by caravan all the way across the deserts from India and China. Jewelry was very important to us. It meant wealth, although actually we didn't wear very much of it because on our kinds of clothes there was really no place for it. Sleeves covered your wrists and would hide bracelets. Dresses were high on your neck and hid any necklaces. We kept most of our jewelry in chests, except for brooches which we used to fasten our clothes. Buttons hadn't been invented yet."

"What did you wear when it was very cold?"

"Usually a full-length straight wool dress that completely covered our bosom and ankles over linen underwear. And then a fur cape or a long mantle. Wolf or beaver or otter. I liked otter the most."

I hesitated because it all seemed so exalted, and then asked, "How about ordinary people?"

"In towns, people dressed more or less the way we did, but less expensively. The country folk usually wore just a crude wool tunic and long rough wool leg wrappings, and kept warm with sheepskin cloaks."

"Like me," Elvira said, and laughed.

The picture Matilda had drawn seemed to be almost entirely of older people. I remembered seeing children in paintings who were dressed in adult clothes and who just looked like little people. I asked if they had toys and things.

"Of course, and mostly carved out of wood—soldiers and knights and castles and wooden dolls we could dress, and puppets and marionettes. Hobby horses were one of our favorites. We'd mount them and sally around the nursery pretending we were out hunting or at war. The boys had wooden swords and make-believe helmets and shields, so they could play being warriors. As we got older, there were board games: backgammon and chess and checkers and cards, of course; we were all great gamblers."

"What about pets?"

"We had dogs and cats just the way you do, and especially birds we kept in lovely cages. I had a mynah bird who could speak at least twenty words." Matilda laughed, remembering. "'Hello Matilda, where's my cake, where's my cake?' Then I had a dog whose name was Digger because he was always going down holes after rabbits and badgers. He was a little short roly-poly thing and tough as nails."

Elvira interrupted. "Your Royalty, enough of children. And dogs and cats. You'll be telling us all about horses next and all the riding lessons you had to take, and how when you got older, you had a warhorse. I want to hear how you met and got engaged to William, and then all about your wedding."

"Oh, yes, please," I cried.

Matilda smiled at my excitement. "Incurable romantics, both of you. All right."

The clock on the church's bell tower stopped any further speech. It tolled a slightly clanging five. With a start, I realized I'd gotten so into the world Matilda had lived in that time had slipped by unnoticed. Dad was having someone for dinner and I had to be home to help Arielle get things ready. "Yipes," I exclaimed. "I have to run." And explained why.

"Then off you go," Matilda said commandingly, suddenly every inch a queen. "And fast."

And with that, she and Elvira vanished, and I found myself alone in an empty church. I heard a light musical laugh from someplace, and then there was silence.

I got moving, and with my mind still mostly in the eleventh century, I crossed the churchyard, went through the rickety gate in the surrounding old brick wall, mounted my bicycle, and headed for the big yellow brick house that was our temporary home.

FIVE

The next day, when I got back, it was early afternoon, and I found the church door open, which meant someone was there. Perhaps just the vicar, I thought, and hoped he wouldn't be staying too long. He always took an afternoon nap, I remembered Elvira telling me. I plunked down on Elvira's gravestone and waited.

But it wasn't the vicar. It was just old Henry, who had been putting away prayer books, replacing burned out candles, and sweeping up. He tipped his hat and said "Good day, Miss," and left. I called "Elvira" and waited, and in the warm summer sun must have fallen half asleep, because a "Hello, Alicia," gave me a shock, and I found myself looking at Matilda, seated casually right in front of me on the altar steps, along with Elvira.

"You were falling asleep,' Elvira said. "Myself, I

thought the old guy would never finish up. He's so terribly slow. I guess we'll be seeing him on our side soon."

Matilda sighed patiently. "Do stop, Elvira. He's a sweet old man and does his job," she said, "and that's what counts. "Now, were was I?"

"You were about to meet William," I said quickly, letting my anxiety to hear about her marriage and wedding burst out of me.

Matilda laughed. "Ah, yes. William," she began. "Well, I was fifteen, not yet your sister's age, Alicia, and considered a real catch. I was pretty, I was well educated, but there was something far more important than that. Marrying me would mean an alliance with my powerful and wealthy father, and Flanders was the envy of many in France, not just in the German Federation. So my father cast around among leading rulers to see where he could make the best deal."

I didn't think I'd heard right, and blurted out, "Your father? But what about *you*?"

"What about me?"

"Well, I mean, what if you didn't love the man?"

Matilda smiled indulgently. "Love? Alicia, in my time, love never came into it. Marriage was a contract between two families or states for political or economic reasons. Most women were married off when they were thirteen or fourteen, some the day they were born. Many never saw their husband until they were brought before the altar."

"But that's awful," I protested. "Couldn't a girl refuse?"

"No, she couldn't. Her father's word was law. Of course, if he loved her, as my father loved me, he might yield to her wishes for a while, but not forever. And if a future husband really horrified her, she could always seek refuge in a religious order and take vows. Few did because that meant living the cloistered life of a nun. It was almost better to be married to the devil himself."

Matilda could see how shocked I was and held up a slender hand, touching three fingers in turn. "In the middle ages, Alicia, a ruler's power depended on three things: they were *land*, then *gold*, along with silver and jewels, and finally *daughters* he could marry off to bond with those who would be useful as allies. But truly, it wasn't always as bad as it sounds. Once married and able to bring new life into the world, we were revered as being in the image of the beloved Virgin Mary, and we were often given extraordinary power. Among the nobility, we controlled the manners, behavior, and education of everyone in our castle, from our children and the gentlemen and ladies of the court to the lowliest servant. We were responsible for everything everyone ate and drank. Most importantly, because we were usually far better educated than the men, many of us were looked to by husbands for serious counsel and advice."

Elvira broke in. "Matilda's forgotten to say that when her father started looking around, the suitors lined up from the Russian forests to the Atlantic Ocean because she was considered the most beautiful princess in all of Europe."

Matilda said, "Shush. That was just gossip." But I could have sworn a blush of pleasure appeared on her ghostly pale cheeks.

"At the time," she went on, "I had a terrible crush on a young English lord who spurned me and broke my heart, so I wasn't in the mood to say yes to anyone. It was no to whomever, no matter how powerful. Fortunately, I had the kind of father who was patient with me, although I drove the dear man nearly to despair. 'You'll soon be too old,' he would cry.

"Then one day that I shall never forget, an envoy appeared from Normandy, one of the most powerful kingdoms in Europe. He brought a letter from William who, as its seventh Duke, was considered the most powerful of warriors anywhere and certainly one of the most handsome. William offered a treaty that would have put my father in a very strong position against Henry, the King of France, as well as against the emperor of the federation. Both were jealous of my father and itched to get their hands on Flanders, with all its wealth. In turn, a treaty would have vastly benefitted William, who was constantly fending off the French king as well as the Duke of Anjou, ruler of a wealthy kingdom to his southwest.

"But William? I was scandalized. I angrily told my father 'No.' I was not going to marry a bastard, especially not that Norman one."

Seeing I was puzzled, Elvira quickly explained. "William was *bar sinister*, you see, and wore a red stripe that ran diagonally across his shield to show it. Many of the knights and rulers in Europe were *bar sinister*."

"It meant they were illegitimate, and there wasn't any stigma attached to that," Matilda said, "But William was different because of his mother."

"His mother? What had she done?"

"She was the low-born daughter of a tanner whom William's father had been adulterous with. You couldn't get lower than that."

"What was a tanner?"

"A tanner," Elvira said, "skinned slaughtered animals, cattle and sheep and goats, and cured their hides to make leather for shoes and belts and things. He was forever covered with blood and smelled terrible."

"Birthright meant everything in my day, Alicia," Matilda said. "You were born and lived in your class and no other one. Nobility married nobility, bourgeois married bourgeois, peasants married peasants. I was a direct descendant from the great Emperor Charlemagne as well as from Alfred the Great of England. I could have suffered William's Viking blood; his great, great-something grandfather had virtually stolen Normandy from the French Kings in exchange for not sacking Paris."

She didn't have to say more about Vikings. I'd read about them in school. They were the scourge of Europe for centuries: brutal warriors who came in long boats out of Scandinavia, armed to the teeth and dressed in furs with horns projecting from their helmets. They struck terror everywhere they went, looting and stealing and murdering.

"But a tanner's grandson?" Matilda said. "I personally told the envoy I would die before I would marry William, and further I said precisely why. To make certain he took that message back to William, I wrote it down and stamped our royal seal over my signature.

"Well, I was young and stupidly proud and foolish. I thought that would be the end of it. I didn't know William. I didn't know the deep humiliation he had always felt about his mother's birthright. I didn't know how all his youth he had suffered the taunts of the barons he would have to overcome to assume the dukedom that his father had willed him before going to die on a crusade in the Holy Land. I didn't know of the whispered laughter behind his back by all the royal court of France. You see, when William's father went away, he gave William to King Henry of France to raise, since Henry was William's godfather and a close friend and ally. And I hadn't heard that William had mercilessly put to the sword an entire town he was laying siege to when its defenders hung the hides of animals from the walls to taunt him. But I soon found out. Oh, yes."

Matilda smiled wryly and shook her head. "I found out about William's humiliation one glorious spring day a few months later. I had gone out into Bruges on my palfrey, a lovely snow-white mare, a gift from my mother, accompanied by my ladies-in-waiting and a small armed guard. It had rained several days before, and the streets were a fetid quagmire from oxen and horses, dogs and cats, and people as well. But we were used to that sort of thing and were safe from it up on our horses. We had just crossed a little bridge over a small stream and were walking slowly down a straight stretch between rows of small houses when I heard a shout behind. I turned to catch a glimpse of a tall dark-haired rider bearing down on me, past one of my fallen guards, and the other guard at swords with a second rider.

"Just a glimpse. The next thing I knew there was the most violent jerk on the two long braids I always wore. I was lifted by them off my palfrey and thrown into the disgusting mire face down. I felt the first blows rain across my back and rump. My head was jerked up and slammed down into the filth of the road again and again. A man was roaring, 'Flanders bitch! Call me a tanner's bastard, will you!'"

"More blows, and all the time the screams of my ladies. Then suddenly the shouts of men, and I was freed from the weight of William holding me down. For it was William, all right, the famed Duke of Normandy himself. I struggled and got to my knees just in time to see a knot of my father's knights bearing down on my assailant and his companion. They were seconds too late. The two Normans were back on their horses and in full flight.

"I was taken home, bathed, consoled. Herbs and mustard were applied to my bruises. I was given mulled wine to wash the filth from my mouth and to drink. And bit by bit the astonishing story unfolded of William's wild ride with a companion nearly two hundred miles from Normandy to Bruges the moment he got my refusal letter and his flight back to safety in Normandy, pursued by a dozen of my father's knights. Of course, my outraged father immediately declared war on him."

Matilda stopped and laughed. "You know, looking back, I find the whole thing very amusing."

I found myself staring at her with my mouth open and with a zillion questions to ask. "But, but you married him anyway?" I stammered.

"I did indeed. My father and William faced off in one stupid battle after another that got them no place, until one day my father saw the folly of it and called for a truce. William agreed, and then, nothing daunted, sent a renewed offer of an alliance with a request for my hand. If people were surprised by his audacious demand again for me as his bride to seal it, they were stunned at my response."

Matilda paused, smiling. Then, "This time, I said yes."

Even though I knew she had married William—because that was history—I didn't know she'd agreed to it. I was floored. "You said, *yes*?" I echoed. "Voluntarily? After what he'd done to you?"

Matilda nodded. "I had my reasons. My father was hard-pressed by the emperor, who had amassed a large army and was poised to attack. He desperately needed William as an ally. I adored my father, and it was becoming ridiculous to keep saying 'no' to every suitor, and the alternative would be to end up in a convent. That's what I let people think. The real reason was none of that. The real reason was this: I thought to myself that any man who had the nerve and passion to ride nonstop for two hundred miles to attack me right outside my father's house—well, he made any other suitor look like a mewling infant."

"Of course," Elvira said, "the fact that he was considered by every woman in Europe to be the best catch ever had nothing to do with it."

Matilda laughed again. "Good heavens, wherever did you get that idea?"

I still found it almost impossible to understand. I couldn't match any of William's savagery with pictures I'd seen of people in those long-ago days and with the way Matilda had described the beautiful gowns the women wore and all the manners of court life involving the page boys, the gentlemen and ladies-in-waiting, the hordes of servants.

Once more I wondered if I was dreaming all this. Facing me, just a few feet away, were two women who a day or so ago I'd never known existed, one of them a famous queen of England. So once more, I simply stared, still only half believing, until very, very faintly from far overhead I heard the whisper of a passing jetliner, and I knew I wasn't dreaming. Matilda and Elvira were very real.

My curiosity bubbled up again. "How long was it, then, before you were actually married?"

"Nearly three years,"

"Misery! Why so long?"

Matilda had suddenly stood up. "I'm being unexpectedly called upon to return, Alicia, so will you forgive me if why there was a delay waits until next time?" And with a warm smile, she promptly vanished, leaving only Elvira, who couldn't help giggling at my surprised expression.

"You ought to be used to us appearing and disappearing by now," she chided.

"But what did she mean about being 'called upon'?"

"We have rules, like anybody else. We're allowed so much time in the 'life' world. Matilda was so enjoying herself that she clean forgot she'd overstayed."

Just the same, I felt a flood of anxiety. "But will she be back?"

"But of course, silly." And with that Elvira also simply vanished too, and there was only the fading sound of her laughter, which in the old church was suddenly kind of eerie.

That's when I suddenly spooked out. Not from the ghosts. Not from Elvira and Matilda. It was the church itself. It was so silent. And so empty. And, because of the time, the daylight that came through the stained glass windows was now beginning to fade. The vestry door was half open, the vestry beyond it dark, and I expected that at any moment a real person would appear from the vestry or from behind one of the stone columns holding up the stone roof arches. I think I would have died if there'd been someone, and I didn't wait to find out. About a second later, I was on my bike, and headed back home.

SIX

My anxiety over how Matilda had simply upped and disappeared was gone the moment I saw her again. I'd hardly sat down on Elvira's fallen gravestone, which was warm from the bright sun, when there she was, Elvira too.

Matilda right away got into the business of her wedding being delayed three years.

"First," she said, "there was William's usual trouble at home. That meant Anjou. The count wanted Normandy for himself, and constantly attacked. Then there was Henry of France. The King saw an end to his dreams of conquering Flanders with my marrying William, so he persuaded the pope to forbid our marriage on the grounds that William and I were cousins, even if very remote ones."

By this time I'd managed to stop worrying about asking too many questions. "Henry again," I exclaimed. "But you said he was William's godfather and had raised him."

"He was indeed, but Flanders's wealth blinded him to that."

"And then the pope? How could he forbid your wedding?"

"The pope was Christ's vicar on earth, the representative of God himself. Step out of line and he or one of his bishops could excommunicate you. That meant denying you God's mercy in life so that you'd be tormented forever by demons in a fiery hell when you died."

I couldn't hide my incredulity. "Did people really believe all that?"

"Absolutely. It was as real to everyone as, say, your father and sister are to you."

"Awesome. So the only person safe, then, was the pope."

Matilda smiled. "Not quite. Even the popes had weaknesses. The Vatican wasn't a little place like today, Alicia. It was a wealthy state half the size of Italy, and there were always those who wanted it, so the popes often were in need of help from one king or another. They had to think twice before abusing their power. And there you have the whole history of Europe until well past my time. Who would run things? Who would determine the present or future of everyone's life? The kings or the popes?"

"Some of the popes were horribly wicked," Elvira said. "One had his castle bedroom directly over the torture chamber and would lie awake at night laughing at the screams of his victims."

I must have looked as shocked as I felt because Matilda quickly said, "Popes weren't like they are now, Alicia. Some stole, others murdered and made war, some were married, and many had children, married or not. One pope even ran a brothel. Don't ask me how Europe survived them.

"Anyway," she continued, "we managed to get the Pope to relent by promising I would create and endow a convent and William a monastery."

"But engaged for three years," I protested. "How often were you and William able to get together?"

"We didn't. Not until the day before our wedding when William and I, surrounded by courtiers and knights, were introduced briefly in a castle in the small county of Eu, which lay between Normandy and Flanders. The wedding was held there to avoid any argument as to who had the right to hold it. The castle had its own chapel that was especially lovely."

"And you hadn't seen him since he beat you up?"
"No."

Remembering Matilda's description of lying face down in a putrid ditch with William raining blows, I started laughing in spite of myself.

"That's weirdsville," I said. "'How do you do, Mr. Husband. Nice to see you again. Excuse me while I get the mud out of my mouth.' What did you say to him?"

"Very little. We both signed some very official papers, and I had to guarantee *dowry* at the chapel door before I could enter."

"What was a dowry?"

"A dowry was what I would bring into the marriage, and was a substantial part of my father's treasure. Then I also had to guarantee return of my *dower*, which was a third of William's property and which was to be mine during my lifetime only. When I died, it would revert to him."

I began to feel pangs for Matilda. No matter what she said about William, it sounded like she ended up like everybody else back then: married off for politics.

I said so, and Matilda laughed. "True, but guess what," and she positively glowed at the memory. "When I was standing at the altar with William before the long wedding ceremony began, he looked down at me and smiled. It was such a warm and protective smile that all of a sudden I fell madly in love with him, and when I smiled back he fell in love with me. I was the happiest bride in all of Europe. My husband was famous for his temper and his brutal warrior side, but when it came to me, he turned out to be the most loving husband you could imagine. For the whole time we were married he never so much as looked at another woman. Not even after the Conquest, when we were often separated, sometimes for a year or more at a time."

"And in those days," Elvira said, "that was almost unheard of. Fidelity meant nothing at all."

"Exactly. That was in the year 1053. I was twenty-one. William was twenty-four, and we had the most beautiful wedding you could ever imagine. My father brought most of his court and a hundred knights.

The chapel was filled with their banners. And there were his ministers of state and ambassadors, his chief judges and council members. I had a whole crowd of my own, of course, all my ladies-in-waiting, and I don't know how many little page boys. William's entourage was even larger. The chapel was jammed right up to the altar."

"What about your wedding dress?"

"Yes, please," Elvira cried.

"It was every bride's dream." Matilda suddenly seemed much younger to me as she began to describe it. She stood up as though she was modeling the gown, and the way she described it was like a fashion show. I could almost see it.

"I wore a long white velvet gown that was fastened high around my neck, here, with a double string of diamonds and emeralds. It had full sleeves and flared into a full skirt at the waist and nearly covered my feet. My mother and four seamstresses had worked on it for a whole week. I wore satin slippers sequined with pearls, and I had a narrow waistband of roped pearls joined by a silver fastener. I wore no other jewelry except for a silver locket that hung down over my bosom on a slender silver chain. It was shaped like a heart and rimmed with diamonds, and inside it there was a miniature portrait of my mother and father. My hair was in two long braids that fell over the front of each shoulder, and I wore a tight cap of satin banded with silver around my forehead from which hung my white veil."

"But with no heat, weren't you freezing?"

"In one word, yes. But I didn't care. What bride would when marrying a famous knight who made even the King of France tremble?"

She sat down again, and her mood became soft and loving. "And William was so handsome. He melted not just me but all my ladies. He wore a golden doublet embroidered with climbing vines and white hose, and he had on golden slippers of the softest leather that covered his ankles almost like boots. He had a short sword in a golden scabbard suspended from a belt encrusted with diamonds and rubies and sapphires, and of course he wore a crown. That was a broad band of silver embossed with emeralds from which rose five points surmounted by knobs of gold."

I was about to ask a bunch more questions when Elvira interrupted. "Matilda, you forgot the little boy."

"Little boy? Oh, yes." Matilda looked surprised, then her expression became radiant as she remembered. "How could I have?"

She rose and stood next to a gravestone. "Pretend this was the altar," she said. "I was standing here, like this. And William here, and the bishop here. We had just started when suddenly a child came right up between us. He was, oh, I'd say about four or five and a ragamuffin from the streets. He looked like he'd never been washed, and his clothes were in filthy tatters. How he ever got into the chapel no one knew. But all of a sudden, there he was, standing right here between William and me, barefoot and shivering with cold. With the most earnest expression on his little face, he held up to me a small bouquet of wildflowers.

"You can just imagine the gasp from all the guests. The bishop froze, absolutely horrified. You would have thought he'd just seen the devil. Several knights and an acolyte came to life and rushed to seize the boy. But quite expectedly they were stopped by William. In a flash, my husband-to-be bent down, scooped up the child and held him in his arms so that he could hand me the bouquet. When I took it, William kissed him on his cheek, spoke a few soft words to him, then briefly left the altar to hand him to one of his knights with orders to give the child a purse with five gold pieces and take him safely to his parents.

"When he returned to my side, I was too overwhelmed by emotion to speak. This one gesture by the ferocious warrior, with whom I was about to share my life, told me a million things. I clutched the bouquet to my bosom throughout the rest of the long ceremony in a dream of happiness. It took at least three hours, and then there was high mass. My knees ached from kneeling. But when it was finally all over, there I was—married—the duchess of one of Europe's most important states and the wife of its handsome and famous Duke."

"Wow!" I exclaimed. I felt all the excitement of the occasion as though I had actually been there. "What happened next?"

Matilda came back to sit again next to Elvira, who spontaneously hugged her shoulders.

"We celebrated, she said, "for four days and nights. There were hundreds of guests from friendly kingdoms, and in spite of all the trouble he'd caused us, King Henry sent his ambassador and a score of emissaries. What seemed to me half the court of the German emperor came. There was also the papal ambassador and several cardinals, and there were emissaries from the royal family of Castile, which was the very small part of Spain that wasn't Arab. And of course there were any number of counts and dukes who owed allegiance to either my father or William. Over a hundred cooks served them two dozen roast oxen, and a score or more hart."

"Two dozen oxen? Out of sight! What was hart?"

"Hart was our word for deer, which meant the great stags our huntsmen had rounded up. Don't forget—there were no stores. And no refrigerators. We had to grow or kill everything we ate. Meat was terribly important to us because there were no vegetables all winter. A lot of it we had to preserve with salt, so cooks got very good at sauces to play the salt taste down. Then there were dozens of roast pigs, endless lamb and rabbit, and hundreds and hundreds of pheasants."

"You ate all of that?" I asked. The two dozen oxen had really got to me. Oxen are big.

Matilda nodded. "You can be sure we did. Especially since oftentimes there was very little to eat. Even among the nobility. What we didn't eat was given to the poor, who came from miles around to scavenge. We had all sorts of fish, too, from streams and rivers as well as from the sea and prepared in many different ways with all sorts of spices and herbs. There were great drums of wine—an ocean of it. My father had searched all over France and Germany for the very best. I remember one night when I drank far too much of it, and my ladies had to put me to bed."

"For shame," Elvira teased.

"That's what my father said, but there was nothing he could do about it. I didn't belong to him anymore. I belonged to William, and William just kissed me and laughed. And then," she continued, "there was all that pastry."

"Pastry? Really? Back then?"

"Oh, absolutely, and some of it more delicious than anything you can buy today. My father had brought in some famous chefs from Italy for that. And while we ate, there were acrobats and jugglers and jesters and trained bears and apes that did tricks. I remember one ape got loose and was running around on the roof beams, throwing things down at the guests."

Elvira giggled. "I hate to think what else he might have done up there."

"Shush." Matilda put her hand over Elvira's mouth and rolled her eyes at me.

"How about the music?" I asked.

"It was endless. We had teams of musicians with lyre and lute and drums, and every night we danced until dawn. And, of course, there were presents. William gave a magnificent jewel-encrusted solid-gold drinking cup to every single one of his barons and to my father's, too. And my father presented all of William's knights with engraved silver plate. For my wedding present, William gave me a large golden box sculpted all around with flowers and dancing nymphs and filled with every precious jewel imaginable. And not only that, but also several of the most beautiful falcons, with an experienced falconer."

"Falcons? What were they? Birds, right?"

"They were a very special bird, a hawk used for hunting, which was my favorite sport. They killed other birds: partridge, pigeon, quail, and pheasant, and small game, too, like rabbits or badger and squirrel. Only royalty had falcons. The nobility had lesser hunters: the goshawk, for example, for dukes and down the line to the peasantry, who only had kestrels. Falcons took months to train, and the falconers were well paid and enjoyed many privileges."

"Crazy. What did you give William?"

"I gave William six rare Arabian horses my father had brought from the Kingdom of Lombardi in the north of Italy."

Elvira giggled. "If I'd been there, I could have given you one of our plough horses."

Matilda hugged her and went on. "And of course there were all the presents we both received from the guests, most of them jewelry or silver and gold. William's knights gave him a magnificent new suit of armor made in Castile by one of the greatest armorers in Europe. I was given endless bolts of rare cloth, silk and taffeta and wool. You couldn't buy dresses in my day. You had to have them made or make them yourself, so cloth was really important to have."

"But none of that," Elvira said, "could compare with the home William brought you to. Tell Alicia about that."

Remembering, the older woman's eyes again filled with delight. "With all the trouble he'd had," she said, "William's first thought was to protect me and the family he expected us to have. He had ordered a magnificent castle built on a hill above the town of Rouen and the river Seine, which came from the south beyond Paris and flowed north into the English Channel. You could see all the surrounding country-side for miles around from it—all the farms, the villages, everything. Best of all, the castle was almost the very first stone castle in France. I learned that a thousand men had been employed for three years building it. The donjon, the big square center tower, was four stories high. Besides the stables and all the buildings in the bailey that housed the kitchen and forge and the granary and quarters for domestics and soldiers, there were paddocks for the horses to gallop about in and vegetable gardens and orchards, and a special courtyard for me and my ladies, where we could retreat and read and do our needlework in the summer. The high *palisade* surrounding it all was wide, so soldiers could run along it to places they were needed if we were attacked. The castle's living part for William and me and all our attendants was actually in the donjon itself, instead of in the surrounding wall like most other castles, which William said always put families right in the thick of fighting if attacked."

Matilda paused, collecting her memories, and when she continued, her whole expression had changed. Her eyes shone like a child's seeing something magical. She said, "For me that castle was fairyland. I don't think I had ever felt an emotion like the one I felt that day when I rode up to it surrounded by a company of knights, each carrying a colorful banner at the end of his lance.

"The main hall where I would eat and hold court was a huge room two stories high that took up nearly a whole floor of the massive tower. Its ceiling was the roof, which was supported by oaken beams twice as thick as your body. All along one side was a long trestle table of pasture oak where people gathered for every occasion, from meals to official functions. Over the stone fire platform in the center of the room was a great iron cauldron suspended from an iron tripod. Decorating one wall were copies of all the shields of William's barons and knights, each shield painted with the owner's coat of arms. High on another wall was a long row of their banners. Off the main hall, there were screened-off places for William's chamberlain and steward and some of his knights, along with a dormitory for my ladies-in-waiting and latrines and a pantry. Two lower floors served as store rooms and quarters for household servants."

"Where was your room?"

"William's and my bedroom was in a balcony at one end of the main hall. Up there, I also had a second special room all of my own where I kept my clothes, and where I could sit during the day with my ladies and get away from all the people and noise in the main hall. Besides, by nightfall the hall's stone floor would usually get foul and smell terribly, what with the dogs and cats forever soiling it and all the rotting discarded food."

"Oh, yuck," I muttered. I remembered some movie where the people seated in a castle simply threw on the floor whatever they didn't eat.

"Yuck, indeed," Matilda agreed. "Almost the first thing I did, once I'd assumed my duties, was to order the whole room swept out every day and the floor washed before being covered with fresh rushes. In my special room up above, William had hung the walls with tapestries against the cold. He'd also fitted its archer's apertures with windows. Glass had been brought all the way from Italy and mounted on heavy frames set into the stone with iron hinges so that the windows could be opened and closed. You couldn't see much through the glass—it was filled with bubbles of air—but it kept out some of the winter cold, and at the same time, during the day, let in light. That's where I had my children.

"In our bedroom, there was a great bed of four posts with a canopy and heavy curtains to draw all around it which, besides the cold, shut out most sound in the castle. It had a base of tightly webbed rope and a thick mattress filled with goose feathers. For winter warmth, we had covers of ermine and sable and silver fox. We really needed them because back then everybody, including kings and queens, went to bed naked. Night clothes hadn't yet been thought of. And there was an iron brazier that was always kept full of red-hot coals. Before I went to bed, a servant would warm the bed with a covered copper pan filled with coals. William spoiled me terribly."

"What about closets?"

"Closets? We didn't have them in my day. Nor dressers or bureaus. We kept all our clothes in ornately carved wooden chests. I had two of them. The only other furniture in our bedroom was a table and two wooden chairs. There was a large crucifix on the wall over our bed and several paintings on wood of the Virgin mother on the wall."

I didn't even hint that I thought it didn't sound very cozy. Instead I asked about bathrooms.

"Oh, there weren't any of those, either. Just like there wasn't any heat. There were latrines, which were small rooms built into the donjon's outer wall. There was a stone shelf like a bench with holes cut into it that you sat over. Waste dropped down to the bailey below where it was collected for disposal."

Elvira suddenly began to giggle. Matilda turned to her. "What are you on about now, young lady?"

"I heard there was a castle in Switzerland," Elvira managed to say, "where, as punishment, if they got out of line, page boys were chained at the bottom of the latrine shaft where the waste landed."

Matilda managed to hide a smile behind a disapproving frown. "Elvira, do stop with such nonsense."

"But it's true," Elvira said.

Matilda assumed an air of patience, and waited for her to stop laughing.

I tried not to imagine that or any other part of castle living. I could only think how terribly uncomfortable life must have been. Remembering how, when Matilda was a princess, water for washing or drinking had to be hauled up in buckets, I asked, "What about water?"

"The donjon had a deep well inside. Every castle did. If attacked and besiege, you couldn't survive without water. For personal use it was brought up to each floor through a shaft with a rope run through pulleys."

That was a slight improvement, I thought. At least the servants didn't have to cope with lugging heavy buckets up stairs or ladders. I asked about the kitchens.

"They were outside in one of the wooden houses in the bailey."

"Outside? But wasn't the food always cold when it reached the table?"

"Usually," Matilda admitted, "although it could be reheated in the pantry just off the main hall. And of course, most of the time, unless it was a very important dinner, we just ate the thick soup which simmered constantly in the big cauldron in the middle of the room. Everything was tossed into it: meat, chicken, vegetables, bread, even fish. What wasn't eaten each day was left in the cauldron and added to for the next meal along with spices and herbs. Sometimes it was delicious and sometime it wasn't."

I thought *yuck* again and that most of the time it probably tasted awful, but I kept that to myself.

Elvira wanted to know if it was true that they didn't have forks or even spoons and ate everything with their hands.

"It is true," Matilda admitted. "We didn't have

plates either. We put solid food on slabs of unleavened bread we called *trenchers.* Soup or slop went into a big wooden bowl which you took turns drinking from with the person next to you. If you wanted something solid that was floating in it, you just pulled it out with your fingers."

"They didn't have napkins, either," Elvira said to me, "so you can imagine all the dribble down their chins and onto their clothes." She winked and added, "Matilda once told me she'd pulled a dead mouse from the soup."

Matilda said, "Elvira, stop it. You make us sound like savages."

To me, it sounded as though eating in those days was worse than savage. It sounded dreadfully unsanitary. Once again, I tried to reconcile all the hardships of Matilda's medieval life with all the fine clothes, the gold and silver and jewelry, and servants rushing to do everything for her.

I couldn't, and said so.

"It must seem that way," Matilda answered. "But the cold, the food, the vermin—we were constantly ridding ourselves of fleas and lice—all that was the same for everyone, not just me. We didn't know anything else, that was just the way things were. I had an adoring husband, and eventually I was the Queen of England and had the delight of eleven children."

"Eleven?" I could hardly believe my ears.

"Five in Normandy and six after the Conquest." Matilda didn't try to hide the pride in her voice. "And furthermore, two became kings of England."

I found myself almost disbelieving. How on earth had she managed? I said, "But how could you? I mean, I thought they didn't have hospitals then."

"We didn't. We had midwives and other women to help—if we were lucky. And I was. I had a bed, too Most peasant women didn't have either. Half the time they brought a child into the world alone, lying on straw or rushes laid out on the floor."

"Weren't there any doctors at all? And what about medicine? And milk for babies?"

"Doctors were only for the rich and the nobility. And most of them knew far less about medicine than you do. They thought that sickness was carried in the blood by bad *humors* and that getting rid of blood would help you recover. So, if you were sick, they almost always bled you. That meant putting leeches on you to suck out your blood or cutting open a vein. As for medicine, more often than not they would hang a dead frog around your neck, or a poultice of chicken innards, or burn some evil-smelling something in a fire in your room. But again, I was fortunate; I was almost never sick."

"But how did you manage with bottles and all?" I asked. "I mean for the babies. How did you keep things sterile?"

"We didn't. We didn't even know what sterile meant. We had no idea about germs or bacteria. When the plagues hit us, most people thought it was punishment from God. As for babies' bottles, they didn't exist. A mother provided her child's milk herself. If for some reason she couldn't, the child was turned over to another woman who could. Where we nobility were concerned, it was always to someone of our own class. We thought the milk of a commoner would contaminate the blood of a child born noble. I always had milk enough, however, and I nursed all eleven of my darlings myself."

A somberness crept into Matilda's voice. "For all the wonder of marrying William, however, I soon found I had married into a hornets' nest."

"Oh? What happened?"

The words were hardly out of my mouth when there was the sound of the Church door's big iron hinges. The door opened and both Matilda and Elvira disappeared in a flash.

It was the vicar. Coming out, he spotted me. "Ah, young lady. Here again, are you? That's nice. It may rain, though. Don't be out in it and catch a cold. I'll be coming back after tea to prepare tomorrow's sermon, but I suspect you'll be gone by then." Smiling benignly, he continued on his way. The rickety old gate in the mossy brick wall creaked shut, and there was silence. I called Elvira and Matilda but there was no answer. I followed the vicar's footsteps out of the churchyard my head filled with images of life in a medieval castle.

SEVEN

Quite late that same day, I went back to the church. It was after dinner and the sun was sinking low over the Thames. The vicar was there, but he didn't stay long. I'd hardly settled down in one of the pews and pretended to sketch when he left, and Elvira appeared at once. She was seated on the steps up to the altar along with Matilda, even though I hadn't called them.

"We were just waiting for the vicar to leave," Matilda said.

Elvira had the giggles because she had decided that one day she was going to materialize right next to the vicar while he was giving his sermon.

"Don't you dare," Matilda said. "That's against all our rules, and besides, he's too old to be scared."

Elvira pretended to be chastened. "Yes, ma'am, your royalty."

Matilda rolled her eyes in mock despair, smiled knowingly at me, and said, "To answer your question about why I said I'd married into a hornets' nest, William's whole youth from the time he was an infant had been one of defending himself against all those who wanted the dukedom of Normandy for themselves. Countless times, as a young boy, he'd had to flee for his life and hide out with peasants. As a grown warrior, he was endlessly at battle. We'd hardly been married a week when King Henry of France invaded with a large army."

"King Henry? Not *again*."

"I know, but in Henry's eyes Normandy had become a glittering prize with which no loyalties or family ties could compete. He'd incited William's forever rebellious nobles to join him with huge bribes of gold and promises of valuable land, and that made it doubly difficult to defeat him. It was also particularly hard for me because my mother was Henry's sister. I found myself caught between my husband and my family."

"How did you cope with that?" I asked.

"I coped," Matilda said. "When you married, no matter how much power you had in your own right, you still belonged to your husband."

I hardly heard her. I found myself imagining, through the mist of a thousand years, how all of Europe back then was like a chessboard with armed men, instead of chess pieces, forever fighting and betraying everyone else no matter who they were. How had anyone survived?

"What did you do," I asked, "when William went off to war?"

"Well," Matilda replied casually, "If I wasn't busy having a child, I went with him. And sometimes even then."

For a moment, I thought I hadn't heard right. Pictures I'd seen in London of armored knights hacking and slashing at each other with swords and maces and axes and bloodied speared bodies crushed by warhorses didn't fit with the tired-eyed woman, in a way so like a schoolteacher, who sat quietly in front of me, nor certainly with the woman who'd worn beautiful clothes and jewelry and who had looked so slender and alive when she'd described her bridal dress, and who had been the mother of eleven children.

I was hesitant to ask my next question because I liked Matilda the way she was. I wasn't sure I wanted to picture her in battle.

"Did—did you wear armor?"

"Of course: chain mail over a heavy leather tunic, a helmet, and a shield. It was all terribly uncomfortable, and the sword was awfully heavy."

'Did—did you ever used it?"

"Occasionally, although I didn't like to kill people. William always made me stay at the rear of the fighting where he planted his banner, and the enemy used to try to capture it and me with it, so it was me or them."

As I tried to swallow that one, Matilda suddenly smiled. "But you mustn't think it was all endless bloodshed. We had some wonderfully peaceful years, too. William thought business and commerce as important as agriculture. He encouraged foreign trade and turned the town of Cherbourg into the most important seaport of all France, perhaps even of northern Europe. And then, too, town life wasn't at all like peasant life in the fields. Our towns were beehives of activity. There was a trade for nearly everything made, from wagons to jewelry. Trades were organized into guilds a little like your unions, and many of the burghers were wealthy and lived in comfortable homes with servants and good food, and dressed in fine clothes."

"But how about you?" If not at war, I couldn't imagine her sitting in her garden in the castle's bailey doing embroidery and gossiping with her ladies-in-waiting.

"Me? Well, I tried to raise the cultural level of Normandy, starting with my husband's court, which had to set a standard for the rest of the country. Sadly, it had been too long without a woman's hand and was totally lacking in proper manners and ceremony. I soon put that straight. I had always loved architecture, so I had many chapels and churches built to help inspire greater devotion." She laughed. "As you know, you're sitting in one I had built years later. At the same time," she continued, "I encouraged women everywhere to better educate themselves. Since monasteries were the only places you could learn languages and philosophy, I supplied their libraries with important books wherever I could find them and invited leading philosophical and legal minds from the great centers of learning in Rome and Germany to come and teach."

"What about your children?" I asked. "I mean, with no schools."

"They learned the same way I did," Matilda replied. "I found monks and priests, learned men of letters, and I helped, the same way my own mother had with me."

She smiled fondly, remembering. "Our children were a constant joy to both of us, especially William. He loved children. I'd seen that at my wedding when the little ragamuffin came to me with a bouquet. Unlike most fathers back then, he involved himself in every aspect of our children's lives. They often went with us on official visits to other kingdoms. This was unheard of. I'll never forget our visit to the French court in Paris for some momentous occasion and at a time when we weren't warring with Henry. We came into the great council chamber where the King sat, surrounded on every side by council members of high rank in all their robes of state and with heralds blasting away with trumpets to announce our arrival. Up the red carpeted aisle we went between rows of foreign dignitaries from all over Europe toward the throne, but not alone, mind you. Oh, no. We had with us a positive gaggle of clamoring little towheads, and William seemed utterly oblivious to the shocked expressions on the faces of everyone."

I couldn't help but clap my hands in delight. "I love it," I cried.

Elvira, who'd been silently thoughtful, her mind

elsewhere, broke in with a question. "Matilda, when did William start seriously to think of conquering England?"

Matilda grew thoughtful in turn. "I think," she said, "I think it actually was even before we married, although until 1065 he rarely, if ever, spoke of it."

It had darkened, and I realized I could hardly see either Matilda or Elvira. I didn't like biking in the dark, and I was almost relieved when Matilda said, "But we'd better save that for our next meeting. You don't want to have trouble getting home, Alicia. You shouldn't be out on a lonely path at night by yourself."

It was what my mother always said, and I could see myself catching it when I got safely back to our house.

Matilda had hardly spoken when there was an odd flash of light and then a distant rumble of thunder. We were going to get a thunderstorm.

"Oh goodie," Elvira said. "I love thunder and lightning."

"Well, Alicia doesn't, silly. She's not a ghost remember?" And to me, "Alicia dear, hurry. Elvira, come."

I only just made it home before the skies opened up.

EIGHT

When I got to the old Norman church in the morning, to my surprise I found two college-age girls taking rubbings from the inscriptions on several gravestones cemented into the floor right over the graves of the two knights who had been buried under them centuries ago. An iron railing keeps people from walking on them. I had fun telling the girls who the knights were, what they had done, and why they were there. They couldn't figure how I would know such things. It seemed forever before the pair were finished, and then they wanted me to show them sketches I'd made while I waited. Finally, when the old clock in the tower rumbled and its bell struck two, they left with cheerful good-byes. Matilda and Elvira appeared at once and Matilda wasted no time in getting started.

"Alicia, remind me where I left off."

I said, "You were going to tell us when William decided to invade England."

"Ah, yes. Well, you will remember that mine was an age of take what you could, and my dear William was no different from any one else. England was no longer a savage place of warring tribes. By the year 981, it had settled down under Alfred the Great, then after him King Canute, and it had a large, useful population."

"Canute? Was he the one," I asked, "who sat on a beach and ordered the tide not to come in, and it did and soaked him?"

"That's the one. But the tide thing is just silly legend. Actually he was a great king, and by the time he came along, England was immensely rich in agriculture and in all sorts of resources like timber and iron. London was an important city and a great center of learning. The Anglo-Saxons were highly religious, too. The Anglican Church was so powerful that it actually sent missionaries into Germany to convert the pagans there. But with no allies, it was there for the taking *if* you were crazy enough to try. And my William was. Capturing England would make him the most powerful man in Europe. I tried to talk him out of it by reminding him that the Anglo-Saxons weren't people to be taken lightly. They had kicked out the dreaded Vikings. But to no avail."

"Did the English have a big army?"

"They could easily assemble one if necessary."

I remembered seeing movies in which the English were great archers, and asked about it.

"Their famous longbow wasn't around much in 1066. I had one copied from a Scandinavian. I was a good shot, too. I could nail a boar at fifty yards."

"You hunted wild boar?"

"Whenever I could," Matilda said. "For the kill, if my arrow hadn't done the job, I used a spear."

That really flummoxed me. A wild boar, I'd read, could rip the belly out of a horse with one jerk of its head.

"Next to falcons," she continued, "hunting boar was my favorite sport. Actually it was after a boar hunt that William suddenly brought up his English ambition. We'd lost one of our favorite greyhound trackers. The boar attacked it before we could set loose the mastiffs to keep it at bay until it could be speared. The greyhound was the gentlest animal, if not hunting, and slept at the foot of our bed. So we weren't talking much. It was cold and we were tired and hungry and looking forward to a warm fire and hot soup when William suddenly said, "I'm going off to England next week to visit Edward."

"Who was Edward?"

"Edward was the king after Canute. He was known as the Confessor because of his extreme piety. He wasn't well, he'd never had children, and William wanted him to name him as his heir to the English throne. If he did, it would eliminate the risk of invading."

I was puzzled. "Why would Edward want to give his country away to a foreigner?"

"Good question, Alicia. There are two answers.

First, Edward owed William one. As a child he'd had to flee King Canute along with his mother, Emma, who had married the king who ruled between Alfred and Canute. She was William's great aunt, and she and Edward were given refuge for years by William's father. Secondly, William had the ridiculous idea that the English crown was rightfully his, since his great aunt Emma eventually went back to England to become Canute's wife."

Trying to imagine that happening nowadays, I could barely refrain from giggling. It seemed to me that women in Matilda's time were constantly changing husbands.

"I think, however," she continued, "that William just used that 'great aunt' nonsense in hopes of avoiding the enormous danger of invading England. Crossing the channel with a full-sized army was something that had never been done, and I could only think that William's ambition for England would make me a widow."

"So did he go? I mean, visit King Edward?"

"A week later, yes. And, believe it or not, he soon came back with Edward's promise that the throne was his when Edward died. Soon after, just to seal that promise, Harold Godwin came over to declare the approval of England's powerful archbishop and to swear his own loyalty to William."

"Who was Harold Godwin?"

"Harold was the son of England's most powerful earl. He stayed with us for many months, and he and William became great friends. They frequently hunted, and twice Harold joined William in putting down minor rebellions. And, oh, yes. Harold took a shine to one of my daughters and was delighted when William promised her in marriage when she was old enough."

"How old was she then?"

"Seven. Her marriage to Harold would have given William a very trusted lieutenant in England."

I had reluctantly become used to the arranged marriages of Matilda's time and managed not to comment.

"For all their friendship, however," Matilda continued, "William had never quite trusted Harold. He suspected that Harold wanted the crown for himself. So, when it came time for Harold to swear his oath of loyalty, William secretly hid sacred relics under the altar on which Harold placed his sword. This would make Harold's oath holy in the eyes of God. I begged William not to do it. I knew if Harold discovered he'd been tricked into making his oath sacred he'd become so angry that he'd go for the crown himself. Well, I wasn't wrong. When Harold went back to England he persuaded Edward to leave the crown to him instead of William."

"Wow," I said. "That must have shot William a few thousand volts."

"It certainly did. I don't think I'd ever seen him so angry," Matilda said. "For several nights he never slept. He paced up and down, grinding his teeth and choking out the most awful sacrilege. One terrible night he attacked the bedroom itself with his sword.

Mattress feathers flew everywhere like snow. On another, he went after his servants and attendants, knocking them down and cursing them. Adding to his fury was Harold's breaking his engagement to our daughter."

"What did you do?"

"Well, finally I couldn't stand it anymore. After a third sleepless night, I leapt up out of bed, or what was left of it, and screamed at William. "Enough of this, William. Enough. Instead of ranting and raving like some hysterical old woman, do something about it.""

A smile crept over Matilda's face. "Remember that in my day, we slept with nothing on? Well, I screamed so loud that my ladies of the bedchamber and other attendants came rushing in, and there we both were, William and I, stark naked, me shaking with fury, and William, sword in hand. But do you know? It worked. For a moment, William just stood and stared at me, astonished, then at my fleeing ladies and attendants, then at himself, naked with a sword, and then, of all things, he sat down on the edge of our bed and laughed."

Picturing the scene, I couldn't help but giggle, and Elvira and then Matilda joined me. When we all finally stopped, Matilda said. "I could hardly believe it. I put my husband to bed, and he slept like a baby for nearly twenty-four hours. When he awoke he was as calm as a windless sea, and after he'd eaten he went to work. William had decided, for better or for worse, to take the crown from Harold by force. As it turned out, however, what my husband never understood until much later was that in England the crown could neither be inherited, nor could the King name a successor. So neither he *nor* Harold had a right to it."

"Really? Then why did Edward offer it to either of them?"

"Edward was terribly weak. He was probably scared of both William and Harold but more scared of Harold because Harold was right there in England while William was across the Channel."

"Then who ended up King?"

"Harold."

That rocked me. "Wait a minute. Who? What? Harold? I mean, you just said …"

Elvira laughed. "The Witenagemot."

"The who?"

Elvira hastened to explain. "The Witenagemot was an ancient Anglo-Saxon tribal council made up of leading nobles. It was up to them to say who was to be king."

"And they saw Harold," Matilda added, "as the obvious choice because of his success in war and because, as Edward probably had, they saw Harold as *there* and *available* when William wasn't."

It was a long time before I fell asleep that night, stewing over all the politics of that time and wondering how William actually got across the Channel, which Matilda had promised to tell me at our next meeting. Sure, I could read up on all of it on Wikipedia, but hearing it from Matilda, who had actually been there, was bound to be a lot more interesting.

NINE

"My William wasted no time getting started," Matilda said, "and in seven short months he collected together an army of twenty thousand men—ordinary foot soldiers, and archers, and a thousand of cavalry."

At this meeting in the churchyard, we were seated behind a large granite cross that was shaded by a giant tree where Elvira thought it would be more comfortable for me as it was blistering hot.

I leaned against the cross and it felt cool. "Awesome. Twenty thousand? Where did he get them all?"

"Everywhere. From France, lured by promises of plunder, from my father in Flanders, and some from Germany and as far away as Italy. Many were from William's own barons. He bribed them with promises of land and privilege if the Conquest was successful."

"And he got all twenty thousand over the Channel?"

"It took seven hundred boats," Matilda said. "Every carpenter in Normandy was conscripted. Whole forests were cut down."

I tried to picture boats in those days from studying the Vikings in school and remembered their narrow hulls without decks, their big colored sails, and the ferocious Vikings, with their huge mustaches and tangled beards, manning oars. "Seven hundred? How big were they?"

"As big as we could make them. Some were as long as a hundred and fifty feet and twenty feet wide."

"What about the horses?"

"The horses were blindfolded, and many were hung in slings from frames so they wouldn't thrash about. The boats were also loaded with sections of wooden forts that could be put together when the army landed. The largest boat was the *Mora*, which I secretly had built as William's flagship."

"And you went on that one, right?"

"No. I didn't sail at all."

"You didn't? How come?"

"William couldn't leave Normandy without a ruler, so before he sailed he made me co-regent with our son Robert and with all the power to act on his behalf. The big worry was that Henry of France might use William's absence to attack again."

"Oh, boy. That horrible Henry again!"

Matilda smiled at my expression and tone, which betrayed how I felt about the King of France. "It didn't happen," she said. "William was quite the diplomat when he wanted to be, and he had gained special dispensation from the pope, who excommunicated Harold for breaking his oath. That made the pope an ally Henry wouldn't have dared anger."

"Just the same, weren't you very upset not to go?" Elvira asked.

Matilda's eyes darkened at the memory. "It was very hard," she answered. "When he set sail on the 10th of September, I felt as though I'd been cut in half. I was sick with fear, too. What he planned was so audacious and so mortally dangerous as to be unheard of. The Channel's waters and winds were famous for sinking ships. But the weather was beautiful, and the whole Channel was soon filled with sails.

"But then, guess what? The boats could only sail with the wind right behind them. When the wind suddenly shifted to blow straight at them, the whole fleet had to put in for two weeks at the port of St. Valery, a short way up the coast. There, rumor quickly started that the wind had changed because the invasion was against God's will. Within hours, half the army wanted to quit. William was for hanging a score of men as an example, but at the last moment I came up with an idea. William seized on it and ordered the sacred bones of St. Valery, the patron saint of the port, to be put on display, and prayed to them. Word quickly spread, and soon half the army was on its knees, believing the saint would cause the wind to change back."

"And did it?"

"Miraculously, yes. The ships set sail again on the

27th, only days after we heard that Tostig, along with the King of Norway, who also claimed the English throne because he was descended from King Canute, had landed fifteen thousand men in the north of England and captured the city of York."

Seeing me look blank once again, Elvira's laugh rippled out. "Tostig was King Harold's brother and the bad boy of the family."

"He was also my sister's husband," Matilda added. "He was a loathsome murderous creature who was venomously jealous of Harold. His back-stabbing invasion actually helped us, however. Harold had mustered his army on England's south coast in case William invaded. Because of the delay with the wind change, he decided William wasn't coming after all, and with Tostig an equally serious threat and actually there on English soil, he force-marched his army north in four days to Yorkshire and a place called Stamford Bridge, where he met Tostig and defeated him in a big battle.

"Poor Harold. History feels sorry for him, and rightly. He'd hardly started celebrating his win when he got news that William had successfully crossed the Channel. He had to rush his exhausted troops all the way back down to the southern coast. It was too much for his army. They were defeated in the famous battle near Hastings and Harold was killed."

What Matilda related really made me add things up. The whole future of England and perhaps even America had depended on one battle, and that battle in turn on events most people had never heard of.

I thought of the old saying, *For the sake of a nail a horseshoe was lost, for the sake of a horseshoe a horse was lost, for the sake of a horse a king was lost, for the sake of a king a kingdom was lost.* In Harold and William's case, it had been that close.

I asked Matilda how long it was before she found out.

"I heard a few days later. I was at prayer in chapel. It was a dark day with a chilling rain blowing in from the north. My teeth were chattering from the cold, and I remember hearing an insistent voice saying "Your Highness. Your Highness." When I finally looked up, I saw a young courier, soaked from head to foot, his tunic, boots, and trousers spattered with mud, his beard and matted hair frozen. He fell to his knees and held out a parchment. When I simply stared, the bishop came from the altar and seized the parchment from the exhausted man's hand. One quick glance, and he fell on his knees beside me. 'Your majesty. He lives, he lives. He has defeated the English at a place called Hastings. Harold is dead. William is King of England.'

"The rest is still a blur, but I remember laughing and crying at the same time and handing a small purse filled with gold coins to the poor deserving courier."

"Did you realize then that you'd be a queen?"

"Oh, I never thought of that. I was too relieved and overjoyed to think of anything but that my William was safe and sound."

"It wasn't until Christmas that he was actually

crowned, though, wasn't it?" Elvira asked.

"You're right," Matilda said. "So in a way my relief was short-lived. The crown was William's, but there still was resistance by some, and he had to fight his way to London to claim it." Matilda's expression once again grew somber. "Meanwhile, something came into my life that brought suffering as bad if not worse than what I'd experienced waiting for news of William."

"Why, what happened? Not Henry again?"

"No, for once not horrible Henry. On Christmas Day, a fever plague struck the castle. First it chose some of the kitchen and household servants, then one of my ladies. I was in the nursery playing chess with Robert; Adeliza, my lovely second born, was reading to the younger ones. The moment I heard, I went at once to the poor lady's bedside. She was burning up and past recognizing anyone. I had but one thought—my children! They would have to be removed from the castle at once. But to where?"

Distracted by Matilda's story of the Conquest, I had almost forgotten her children. I wasn't certain how many there were at that time, and asked.

"Starting with Robert," Matilda said, "who was twelve, there were nine. Matilda and Henry hadn't yet been born. Robert, who was very grown up for his age, thought fleeing the castle was cowardly. He urged his brothers and the older of his sisters to stay and face the plague. I had to put my foot down really hard. I grabbed the huge sword William had given me and told Robert to obey or I'd use it on him for the sake of the others. I think I scared him half to death, and it certainly stifled any protest from William Rufus and Richard, who were ten and nine. The child I was most worried for was little Constance. She was an infant, born very soon after William left for England. And Agatha, who was only two. The plague usually carried off children in twenty-four hours."

"The one that got me didn't even give me that long," Elvira said with a wry smile. Then it was her turn to ask a question. "Where did you hide from it?"

"One of my ladies had a large manor house in a shallow valley near the coast. Her husband was away with William, and she offered me the place at once."

"But mightn't the plague strike there also?" I was beginning to feel the fear Matilda must have suffered.

"Yes, but there was an even chance that it wouldn't. The house was completely isolated. There was no village nearby, and the servants there were ordered not to communicate with any of our guards who were bringing us there. They might contaminate them, so they'd be sent back the moment we arrived. Getting there was hard. The wind and rain were bitter. We bundled everyone up in extra clothes and blankets, all except for Robert, and got them into an oxcart—there were no carriages back then. That's when the real struggle began. It took forever, and we had hardly arrived when Adele, who was only four, was struck. I rushed her to bed and sent a servant to a nearby monastery to fetch a monk famed for curing ills with various herbs. I sent another servant to Rouen to summon a learned doctor. I was sure Adele needed to be bled.

"The monk came first. He fashioned some kind of vile-tasting soup from herbs and treacle and the dried powdered skin of a serpent. And he made a poultice of ravens' droppings and fish eggs mixed with crushed nettles all tied up in a linen bag, to lay on her chest to draw out the pestilence. But her fever got worse, so I sent him away. The bleeding didn't work either when the doctor finally came. I was frantic. Clearly her fever was God's will. But she was just a child. Was she being punished for her father's conquest of England? A priest came and confirmed this was so, and told us to beg God's forgiveness. Then William Rufus came down with it, then Adeliza and little Gundred, and finally little Agatha."

Oh, my God, I thought. What a nightmare. I asked how old Gundred was.

"Gundred was three. To make matters worse, a winter storm blew in from the north with sleet and snow. The house was freezing and shook and trembled from the wind, which howled like a hundred wolves. I had all the children together in one upstairs room on mattresses on the floor. I brought up wood myself from the cellars and kept fires going in two large braziers. The servants had all fled except for one very old woman who came to sit outside the door, insisting she could cause the dead to come to life if any child died. She huddled in rags by a tiny brazier of her own, half hidden by filthy old shawls and muttering incantations against evil spirits. I was certain she was a witch and didn't dare drive her away for fear she might curse my children and give them no chance to recover, but I heavy-bolted the door in case she tried to enter.

"A week went by. There was very little to eat. The servants had ransacked nearly all the stores. The children were too sick to eat anyway, but I found a bit of bread and some rancid meat in the kitchen for myself. I was terrified of having the plague strike me also and leave my children on their own. Later I went outside and snared some rabbits and cooked them over the braziers. I also got water from the well, and to make it safe for them to drink, I diluted it with wine I found. I'd heat it just enough to take the bitter chill out of it, and gently bathed the children to try to bring down their terrible fevers. They had trouble breathing, so I took all the rosemary I could find in the kitchen, along with thyme, which they had in great tied-up clumps hanging from a beam. All during several nights, until none was left, I threw handfuls of it onto the hot coals of the brazier so that the essence of both herbs filled the air for my children to breathe in."

Matilda was silent then, lost in the memory of it. The wintery chill of the old church we were sitting in made her freezing ordeal in the empty manor house seem even colder. I was scared to ask the outcome, but I finally did. "How long did it last?"

"It was nearly a week before the fever broke, first with Adele and then William Rufus."

"What about the others?"

"Cecilia came out of it, I think the best. One moment she was burning up and the next, as the fever broke, she was up and walking about, weak, yes, but as though she had never been ill."

Elvira found the courage to ask about the other children.

Strangely, Matilda suddenly seemed coldly detached, as though tired of centuries of remembered grief. "Gundred and Adeliza didn't make it," she said and went on matter-of-factly. "We were there in the manor house until word was brought that the castle was safe. I guess it was nearly a month. So we went home. I was so very tired." She smiled. "I must have been a sight. My clothes were filthy from the children's putrescence and my not being able to wash it away or bathe the whole time. My hair was the same and in tangles. When we came up to the gate of the outer wall, the sentries didn't recognize me. One rudely ordered, 'Get off, foul woman. No beggars allowed,' and shouted to make haste before I'd regret it. Robert saved the day. He leapt down off the oxcart, grabbed the spear away from the man, brought it up to his throat and shouted "Vile varlet! Down on your knees before Her Majesty."

"He was recognized, and it wasn't long before I was in my own suite, bathed and dressed in fresh clothes and reading letters from my husband, who had been informed of what had happened by courier and was frantic. The children were back in the nursery or their own rooms, except for Robert, who, proud of having faced up to the guard, a seasoned veteran of wars, at once went out hunting with some friends."

Matilda broke into slightly self-deprecating

laughter and gave me a motherly look. "And, dear young friend, that was the life of this queen, for a while at least. Can you imagine?"

I could not. I found almost unbearable the thought of Matilda alone with her children and death in a storm-struck empty house and facing a plague with neither medicine nor food nor human hands to help. I asked when she finally saw William again.

"Not until March. He left England in charge of his brother Odo, and when he landed at Cherbourg, I think it was the most wonderful day of my life. All of Normandy celebrated for weeks on end."

"You forgot something," Elvira said.

"What?"

"You forgot to tell Alicia that your husband came home to a peaceful and prosperous state, which was that way only because you managed it so well."

"You're very kind," the ghostly queen said. "I did only have to take up arms once. I found that patience and diplomacy often worked better than force. But there was a plus to William being away. I was able to spend time improving life in Normandy with all my educational and architectural projects. And then, too, we had begun the Bayeux Tapestry."

"What was that?" I asked.

"You don't know about the Bayeux?"

"No."

"Will you be visiting France while you are here?"

I said I wasn't sure but that I thought my father mentioned he'd like to.

"Well, if you visit Normandy, I'm sure your

parents won't want to miss it. It's a tapestry showing the whole Conquest in pictures. I understand they've got it in a glass case in a special museum and …"

A whispered "Hsst …!" stopped her from going on. Elvira held up a warning hand. In the next instant she and Matilda had disappeared.

There was suddenly a lot of noise at the church door and a whole crowd of boys and girls poured in for choir practice.

TEN

That night at dinner, I asked Dad he'd ever heard of the Bayeux Tapestry.

"But of course," he said. "It depicts every phase of the Norman Conquest of England. And if the Norman Conquest hadn't happened, the language you speak, all the laws we have, even our whole way of life, would be quite different. And perhaps the United States might never have become a country at all."

I asked if the tapestry was very big. "I mean, how many pictures does it have?"

"Hundreds," Dad said. "It's like a giant roll of film. It's nearly two hundred and thirty feet long and only a couple of feet wide. For a while historians thought it was done entirely by Queen Matilda. She was the wife of William the Conqueror. But recently it's thought she mostly supervised a whole team of women. It's valuable not just for its story, but because it tells us a lot about what people were like back then—how they lived, the way they dressed, and all that."

While Dad went on with what he knew about the Conquest, I was hard-put to keep silent and not mention what I'd learned firsthand from Matilda herself.

When I rejoined my ghostly friends, it was another rainy day, and we met in the church again. This time all three of us seated ourselves on the carpeted floor by the altar. I didn't waste a minute in reminding Matilda where she'd left off.

"William had defeated Harold, was crowned King of England, and had come back to Normandy," I said. "And you were about to tell me about the Bayeux Tapestry, except Dad told me all about it last night. Dad says historians think it was done by a whole team of women under your supervision."

"The historians are right," Matilda said. "There is no way any one person could possibly have embroidered a whole tapestry of that length, so I enlisted many of the ladies in my court. Just the same, it took a very long time. Every picture in the tapestry has a Latin inscription saying what it represents, and some of my ladies had trouble with that."

"Latin? How did that figure?"

"As I told you, Latin was a universal language. All treaties and legal documents were in it and all religious works as well."

"Are you in the tapestry?"

Matilda smiled and nodded. "In one or two places."

Elvira said, "So with all that, when did you finally get to go to England?"

"Not for over a year. With William home, we spent the most glorious summer imaginable. We toured all of Normandy in triumph with our children and our whole court, including some Saxon noblemen who fascinated everyone with their long blond hair down over their shoulders and their tremendous blond mustaches. That summer, too, in thanks for William's victory, we dedicated our baby daughter Cecilia to the service of God."

I could guess what that meant. Cecilia would spend her life as a nun taking orders from some bullying mother superior. At the same time, I realized that she might also escape marriage to some perfectly odious man she hated.

I was imagining myself in a cold stone convent in Normandy with no heat or running water and with little to eat when I heard Matilda say that like many things in life, it all ended in the autumn. I quickly came to my senses. "Oh, dear. What happened?"

"There was a serious revolt in England, so instead of Christmas with us, William had to hurry back there. He put down the rebellion and then, finding that his English court didn't function very well without a woman's hand, he sent for me, but winter storms made crossing the channel almost impossible, so I didn't go over until right after Easter.

"I'd hardly stepped ashore when I found myself

at Westminster Abby being crowned, and William along with me for a second coronation. It was awesome. We entered the great cathedral to the blare of a hundred trumpets, and the next thing I knew I was on a throne next to William with an English crown on my head."

Remembering what Matilda had said about the church and kings being anointed, which made them chosen by God, I asked her if she had been.

"Yes," she replied. "William had ordered the same ceremony established by the great Charlemagne, and it placed me equally on the throne beside him as Queen as well as his wife. It gave me an importance and power with my new English subjects that no wife of any previous Saxon king had had."

"And that's why she is always considered England's first queen," Elvira explained. "All the previous wives of kings were mere consorts."

"Also, because with the Conquest," Matilda added, "England, as it was under Alfred the Great and Canute, just didn't exist anymore. William and I were governing a brand-new country, and we both had to get busy quickly to make the Conquest work, and we had to be ruthless. The Anglo-Saxon system of government and laws had to be changed or eliminated. Most Anglo-Saxon property was turned over to Norman nobles, as William had promised, for their support. Norman bishops were placed in key churches and cathedrals; scores of Anglo-Saxon women were married to Normans back in Normandy, which made a lot of women flee to Germany and

France or take the veil, with their homes and estates being promptly taken over by Norman women. Within a hundred years, nearly every name in England was a Norman one."

I thought it all sounded like the most awful abuse of human rights. Elvira said, "Just the same, many of us Anglo-Saxons fought hard to return England to Anglo-Saxon rule."

Matilda nodded. "You're right. I had hardly been crowned when William had to face a serious uprising in the north at York. We had gone back to Normandy for Christmas, and I returned with him to quell it. The roads were either in ruin or there were none at all, so we rode. I had a strong *charger* named Victory, which I always rode when I hunted. But it took us over a week. It was bitterly cold and rained constantly. Also, I was heavily pregnant, in my ninth month. We slept in tents, if lucky. Most of the time we crawled under a tree or some bushes and rolled up in blankets, which were always wet and smelly. We went without bathing and ate mostly cold food. We'd hardly arrived in York—I think we'd only been there two days and had already engaged the enemy—when I gave birth to my fourth son, Henry. I remember the baby's very first sight of his father was William, still wearing armor covered with blood, coming into the tent where he was born and where I was nursing him."

I had become used to hearing of the rigors of eleventh-century life, but could still hardly imagine Matilda riding a horse all day in freezing wintertime rain when about to give birth and with no doctors or hospitals anywhere. And, added to that, the terror of William off fighting someplace when he might be killed. I said, "It sounds awful. You must have had a terrible time."

I had the impression that Matilda didn't want to talk about it anymore. The experience must have been even worse than what she described. So when she hurried on, I didn't ask further.

"No sooner was that rebellion put down," she said, "when we got news of a possible invasion by the Duke of Anjou. There was no way William could leave England, so I went back on my own with my court and our children.

"I hated to leave him, of course, but I didn't have much time to think about it. When the cat's away, the mice play. I let the Duke of Anjou know that if he stepped a foot into Normandy, he would face the Queen of England with the whole English nation behind her, and he backed off. I untangled endless legal suits that had arisen during our absence, and I took steps to revive lagging commerce as well as ensure improvements to our ports that William had started. Then, in the middle of it all, I did something really crazy. I went to war."

I sat bolt upright. "You what?"

"Went to war."

"Out of sight! But where? How?"

Matilda and Elvira laughed. "It was like this," Matilda explained. "When my father died, my older brother became count of Flanders. But when *he* died, his widow became regent for his son, who was my nephew. That's when my younger brother, Robert, saw a chance of getting the dukedom for himself, and he invaded Flanders with a sizeable army."

"Wait a minute. He attacked his own nephew?"

"Indeed he did. I was very angry, and went to my nephew's aid with a large force. Henry of France hated Robert and assisted. There were several battles, and we were defeated."

I couldn't believe I'd heard right. "Defeated? You? You must be kidding."

"Yes. Me. And it was especially bitter because my young nephew was killed."

"Bad news!" I exclaimed. "What did William say to that?"

"He was livid. He wanted to crush Robert and conquer Flanders, since it was also my rightful inheritance. He had his hands full in England, however, and I had hardly got home when I was faced with yet another invasion by Henry of France, taking advantage of my loss in Flanders."

I was again appalled. "Henry! What a troglodyte. He'd just been your ally." I had become so used to what seemed the endless treachery of Matilda's time, however, that I wasn't surprised when she just shrugged.

"I had to appeal to William to send me additional English troops to avoid being overwhelmed," she said. "He could only spare a few as rebellion broke out again at York. In spite of my pleas by courier, William lost all patience, and after putting down the rebellion up there, he vengefully laid waste to vast areas of the countryside, burning crops and villages by the score and slaughtering any who raised a finger, as well as many poor souls who didn't. It was something history would always condemn him for. But that was William. This was the man who had thrown me down in the mud, remember?

"In 1072, six years after the Conquest," she continued, "I was back briefly in England before William and I were separated once more. Even in the short time I was with him, we hardly saw each other. William had all the work of the *Doomsday Book* on his hands."

Doomsday immediately sounded ominous. I asked what it was.

Elvira had been long silent up to now. She brightened and explained. "The word *doom* in Matilda's day meant a *record*. The *Doomsday Book* was an inventory of everything in England. It counted every single person and house, every chicken or horse or cow, and even all utensils and tools."

Matilda said, "It was to help William know how much to tax people. It was a trying time," she added. "The thrill of victory had worn off. The endless rebellions and establishing an entirely new government kept William in England most of the time and me in Normandy. Finally there was something else, something far more serious than any of that." Matilda hesitated before she continued, as though even thinking back on it was painful. "I did something incredibly stupid that tore our whole family apart when we'd been so close. The reason for it had already started, like a distant storm, way back when William sailed off to conquer England. I shouldn't have ignored it then, but I did, and I was to regret that forever."

There was such a sudden sadness in Matilda's voice that I felt a chill run through my whole body. What on earth could she have done?

Elvira said softly, "Matilda, maybe you shouldn't tell Alicia."

"Oh, please do," I said.

Matilda said to Elvira, "Alicia, not a little child," and was about to say more when high overhead the church clock rumbled and struck noon. When its resonant sound had died away, her mood changed. "Can you come tomorrow?"

Could I? My heart sank. "I'm not sure," I said.

Matilda said, "Tomorrow will be our last chance to meet."

Her abrupt and unexpected words brought home something I had avoided thinking about—that Matilda had come to the end of her story and that the next time I saw the lovely queen might be the last time.

I could barely find words. "Tomorrow" had made it even worse. Dad had arranged a day out to visit the Cotswolds, and we were leaving at eight thirty, right after breakfast. "But—but why tomorrow? Why not another day?"

Matilda's smile was warm and loving. "Rules." She sighed. "They keep right on, even after you've left life."

"You'll find a way," urged Elvira.

I knew that somehow I would manage it. I had to. I got to my feet. "Sure." And realized that I was speaking to no one. Elvira and Matilda had disappeared.

ELEVEN

I had set my cell phone vibrator alarm for five and tucked it under my pillow, but when it went off I started back to sleep until I suddenly remembered why I'd set it in the first place. It was pitch dark—the sun wasn't due to rise until six or so—and I got dressed as quiet as a mouse, without turning on the light and scared stiff that someone might hear me. When I looked out the window to see if it was raining, I could barely make out the shapes of trees, but it was just a little fog, and there was enough moonlight coming through it so that I'd be able to see. Dad never rose before seven thirty so I had time to spend with my friends. I could only pray they would come.

Getting downstairs I was sure someone would hear me breathing, and before I slipped out the door I waited a minute to make sure nobody had. Outside, the moon through the fog silhouetted the trees in black lines like dark skeletons. I carried my bike a short distance from the house before I got on it to make sure it wouldn't make any noise on the gravel drive. Just before I started downstairs, I'd heard Arielle moan in her sleep.

At the churchyard and going through the rickety little gate and walking past the silent gravestones, I shivered, and not from the early morning chill. In the foggy moonlight, the stones looked like people who had somehow risen from their graves, and I had to remind myself that ghosts couldn't harm me. After all, hadn't I been talking to two for the past month?

"Elvira?" There was no answer. A million reasons Elvira and Matilda wouldn't appear rushed into my head. Perhaps they were visiting someone else somewhere; perhaps they had decided I'd never show up. I called again. Silence. Frustrated, I tried the church door. To my surprise, it was open. Elvira had to have heard me. The vicar never, ever left it unlocked. Inside, there was just enough moonlight coming through the windows to allow me to see. I got out my little bedside flashlight I'd brought along and made my way up the aisle between the pews toward the altar.

"Elvira?" Still no answer. I began to feel frightened. Suppose Elvira hadn't opened the door. All my strange fears of being alone in the empty dark church came back. Suppose there was someone else here besides. My imagination began to run wild. A murderer, maybe? I turned and was about to run when I felt a soft breath of air on the back of my neck that nearly made me scream, and then I heard Elvira's light musical laugh.

"Yipes, Elvira. You scared me silly."

More light laughter, and then Matilda's voice. "We're both here, Alicia. Make your way up to the first pew. Aren't you clever to have got up so early. And don't mind Elvira, she's in one of her moods. Elvira, do behave."

Matilda was sitting on the step leading up to the altar. Still laughing, Elvira joined her, and I plunked down in the first pew. Matilda waited a moment until Elvira stopped laughing, and then asked, "Now, where was I?"

"You said you'd done something awful that almost wrecked your family." I waited, hoping I hadn't been too brash.

It was a moment before Matilda spoke; her mind seemed far away. "Yes. Elvira knows. The Conquest was a success, Normandy was finally calm, and our remaining children were well and growing. And then I nearly ruined it all. Not just William and myself and the children, but even Normandy and the success of the Conquest."

Elvira burst out, "Matilda, that's nonsense. You ruined nothing. It was Robert's fault, not yours."

I couldn't follow this. Who was Robert? With relief I remembered Matilda's brother, with whom she'd been at war, and I said, "Oh, yes. Your brother."

Matilda saw my confusion. "No—no, not my

brother. Elvira means my son Robert." She took a deep breath. "Alicia, do you remember when William departed on his Conquest in 1066 that he made both me and our son, Robert, regents to rule in his absence and that Robert was then only twelve?"

"Yes, of course."

"Because of his age, he was really regent in name only, but as he got older, he began to take his role seriously and get personally involved in much of Normandy's administration. I didn't mind at first. It meant I could finish work on the tapestry and devote myself to other things. I was mistaken. Robert began to see himself as duke instead of his father, and worse, he began resenting his father for resuming charge whenever William was back. First there was sullenness, and then, when Robert's resentment broke out, there were some nasty scenes. William was not a man who could tolerate anyone presuming to take over his rule. I tried to make peace, but I found my voice useless. The castle fast became a gloomy prison.

"Finally, Robert seized on something that brought things to a head. When he was very small, William and I had him engaged to a little girl named Margaret. She was the niece of the Earl of Maine, the province between us and the duchy of Anjou. The purpose was to make Maine a peaceful buffer against Anjou's ever envious and belligerent duke. Well, when Margaret died two years before the Conquest, William saw her death as ending the alliance, and promptly invaded Maine and filled it with troops, so the Duke of Anjou couldn't attack him from the rear.

"Unfortunately, however, my William didn't often read documents carefully. When it came to signing the surrender agreement with Maine, he missed a clause in which Maine demanded that Robert be its earl when he came of age."

I thought I saw what was coming. "And he did?" I ventured.

"Just so," Matilda affirmed. "Robert not only claimed the title but all of Maine as well, and William wasn't having that. He was wrong, and I told him so. He'd signed an agreement, but with William, what he'd taken with his sword he wasn't handing over to anybody, not even his own son."

"Ouch. Or did Robert back down?"

"He did, but it only needed some little thing to set off an explosion, and my younger sons, William Rufus and Richard, provided it. They got it into their fool heads to empty some chamber pots down onto Robert when he was walking directly below them, and Robert completely lost it. My husband, sword drawn, prevented tragedy, but the damage was done. Robert stormed out of Normandy, taking with him a party of young nobles who had come to see him as he saw himself—as the rightful duke.

And I saw a train wreck coming up. "Oh, bummer, Matilda. That sounds bad."

"It was, and it got worse. Robert went to Flanders to his uncle, my younger brother, Robert, with whom I'd warred. Of course, that suited my brother only too well. He incited my son to stir up real trouble for William and me in Normandy, and my son proceeded to enlist more disaffected nobles."

"But wait a minute," I protested. "Why do you feel you did anything wrong?"

"Because I did."

"But what?"

"The worst possible thing in the situation. I don't know what got into me. Robert was my firstborn, and in spite of his behavior, I adored him. So when he ran himself deeply into debt from bribing nobles to his cause, I gave him money."

"Oh, oh. And William found out, right?"

"Unfortunately, yes. And we had a terrible scene. I confessed complete thoughtlessness. I pleaded I had done so only out of love for our son. I begged his forgiveness. But it didn't work. For months we didn't speak. I tried to calm Robert down, too. But to no avail there, either, and it all went from bad to worse. The next thing I knew, using the money I'd given him, Robert was marching on Normandy with a sizeable army and with the King of France by his side."

I felt a wave of anger well up in me. "Oh, stop! Not that awful man again. What was the matter with him?"

"Greed," Elvira stated flatly. "As usual."

"That and jealousy over William's success," Matilda added. "William met them with his own army; it was mostly made up of English troops as he was afraid of disloyalty among his Norman forces."

"But that was almost like England being at war with Normandy," I exclaimed. "And with William king of both."

"Worse," Elvira murmured. "It was father and son at war against each other."

"And there was more horror to come," Matilda said. "Both Richard and William Rufus sided with my husband. So it was father against son and brothers against brother. I was helpless to stop it. In my lifetime, when men got their killing blood up, talk or tears were useless. The two forces met on a plain near Rouen; It was terrible and bloody and cruel beyond words. A great number of brave men died or were maimed for life."

Again remembering paintings I'd seen of medieval battles, I shuddered. "But at least William won, didn't he?"

"No, he didn't," Matilda said sadly. "For the first time ever, William lost a battle. And if that wasn't enough, there was a final disaster. In the melee of knights and foot soldiers, with horses screaming and rearing and wounded men falling or killed, Robert, on horse, didn't recognize his father, who had lost his own horse and was on foot. William saw what was coming, a knight with leveled lance bearing down on him. He tried to leap out of the way, his sword raised to swing. But he was too late. Robert's lance pierced his sword arm through and his sword fell, useless. There was no mercy in battle. Robert leapt down on William, who was now helpless, and would have killed his father right then and there, except at the last moment he recognized him."

"Thank heaven," I cried. "What did he do?"

"Robert? It stopped him cold. Deep down, he adored his father. In his horror at what he'd done, he was devastated. His bitter resentment vanished on the spot. He called off his forces and took William in his arms—he was very strong—and carried him from the field. I was at our standard, holding off two men-at-arms, when suddenly there was deathly quiet all over, and my beloved son appeared with my husband, both of them covered with William's blood. It was a terrible moment. Knights of both sides rushed to help. William was carried back up to our castle and laid on a bed. Physicians were called to stem the flow of blood. His wound was bad, but far worse was the wound to his pride. In all his wars and battles, he'd never once been hurt. And further, to be defeated by his own son while defending his own kingdom?" Matilda shook her head. "No words could describe how he felt. It took weeks for both wounds to heal. The arm first, then William's pride. For a long time, he was so torn by anger and rage that every effort I made to ease his pain seemed hopeless. Bit by bit, I succeeded, so when Robert finally came on bended knee to ask forgiveness, William forgave him."

A faint light had begun to show through the church's windows. The old clock in the church tower suddenly creaked and rumbled and then struck six times. Matilda was silent a moment, lost in memories. What she had recounted seemed so terrible to me that I felt it would be out of place to say anything.

Elvira broke the spell. She managed a smile and forced her usual brightness into her voice.

"Were there any more wars?"

"Not in my lifetime," Matilda replied. Her voice was filled with all the pain of what had happened so very long ago. "William and Robert were at each other again a number of times. But it never was worse than angry words. And William eventually forgave me, as he had Robert. In a few years we were back on our old footing, but you know, once the golden thread of trust is broken, it cannot ever be mended. From our being one person, we had become two, and for the rest of my life I had to live with the truth that I was the one who had caused that. Through all eternity, too, I shall live with the guilt and remorse of it, just as I have these past thousand years."

"Please don't," I said. "You mustn't." And when there was no reply, "Did William go back to England?"

"Yes. Most of the time he was there. He had the task of restructuring nearly every aspect of English life, from laws and commerce to banking. So once again I was running Normandy. We could see each other only occasionally, usually over Christmas and Easter. I would go to London, and I ruled England for a while as the rightful English Queen when William had to come back to Normandy."

"What happened to that awful Henry of France?"

"Henry died and was replaced by a more peaceful king. The same happened to the Duke of Anjou. My daughter Constance, a baby when her father conquered England and who had married the young

Duke of Brittany, she died, too, and that grieved me deeply. Over the years, the leaves of the tree of life slowly yellow and then fall away to the ground. I myself didn't live long enough to see the Bayeux Tapestry finished, nor to see William Rufus become King of England and his younger brother Henry succeed him. I became very ill, and in 1083 the Lord took me from life on earth. And that, Alicia, is my story."

It came as a shock when she said it. I had been so intent on listening that I'd forgotten that my meeting with Matilda was slated to come to an end. I felt my eyes burn and was afraid I was going to cry. That wouldn't do in front of a queen who had been through so much. I fought back the tears and managed to find words. "Thank you so much, Matilda," sounded completely trite after all I'd heard from her about her life.

I fumbled again and finally said, "All the time you were telling it to me, I had a question that I never quite dared ask. Would you mind if I asked it now?"

"Please do."

I tried to think how to say what I wanted in a tactful way, but then decided just to blurt it out. "Well, I always wanted to ask you, what did it *feel* like to be a queen? When you were my age, you didn't know you would be one, did you? And certainly not the first Queen of the England." I hesitated, then stumbled on. "I mean, all that money and power and being able to order everyone around. Was—was there any other *you* deep inside the 'queen' that was more like ordinary people, like—well, like me?" I broke off. Had I gone too far?

Matilda was thoughtful a moment and then said quietly, "In my lifetime, a queen or a king could do almost no wrong. It was a little like being God. People could live or could die because of what I wanted or didn't want, or said, or didn't say. When I became queen, there was also at first the 'me' I always had been, the inner Matilda with her own thoughts and feelings she shared with no one but herself. When I was a princess, that was the little girl who felt wrapped in armor looking out at the world from its protection to see how others reacted to things she did or said. It was the child who struggled to conquer all her lessons—the languages, the science, all the prayers—or who snuggled deep under the furs on her bed at night and dreamed of fairies and angels. That *me* was a person like you, Alicia, someone enjoying a meal or a bath or a book, or music or a beautiful day in spring. And even for a while, as a queen, she was still there.

"But then, little by little, that me lost out to the new outer me, the Matilda the outside the world required and which I slipped into like a hard shell every morning on awakening. More and more that shell eclipsed everything else."

Matilda paused a moment and then said, "What happened to the old inner me, which is what I think you mean? Sadly, much of the time it didn't have the chance to exist. When occasionally it would reappear, I would feel a sudden crushing loneliness and try desperately to keep it with me until it disappeared again, once more at the mercy of the outer royal shell. For some, Alicia, being royalty has a price. Does that answer your question?"

I nodded and managed to stammer some words of assent, hoping that in the afterworld she had managed to regain some of the inner "me" she felt she'd lost as queen.

"Then it is time for us to go," Matilda said. She rose from the altar steps, and when she said, "Come, Elvira," I saw her as every bit the queen she had been.

"Oh, no. Do you have to?"

"I'm afraid so," Matilda said. "Otherwise you might get in trouble." I looked at my wrist watch. It was past six thirty. I was instantly stricken with reality. "Elvira, please, don't you go, too. Am I never to see you again?"

"Perhaps. Perhaps not," Elvira said matter-of-factly.

"Oh, please," I cried. I felt the beginning of tears again and wanted to put out my arms and embrace both the ghostly women, but knew that I couldn't.

"Good-bye, dear Alicia, I've loved meeting you." Even as Matilda spoke, she disappeared.

"Thank you," I called after her. "Thank you, thank you!"

"Good-bye from me, also, Alicia," Elvira said. "And thank you once again for the flowers." She rose from the altar steps and in a flash disappeared.

I couldn't believe what was happening. The world I'd found in the churchyard was coming to an end. Suddenly, I didn't care about getting home on time. I didn't care that I might skew all of Dad's plans. I felt a surge of desperate and angry stubbornness. I had to get Elvira back; I just had to. Somehow. "Please, Elvira, you mustn't leave, too. Come back. You've forgotten something." I believe I actually stamped my foot. "Elvira! It's really important."

Almost to my surprise there was a ripple of light laughter. Miraculously, Elvira appeared quite calmly and as though she'd never left for even an instant.

"What did I forget?"

Numbly, I realized she'd just been teasing. "Elvira! Matilda's right. You're—you're," I tried to remember the word Matilda had called her. "Incorrigible," I said, finding it somewhere in the back of my mind. And then, in spite of myself, I joined Elvira's infectious laughter. "You've never told me about *your* life," I added.

"But I'm not interesting," Elvira said. "I'm really terribly ordinary. I'm just a farm girl."

"Nonsense," I said firmly. "You're not ordinary at all. You're not like anybody I ever knew."

"That's because I'm a ghost." Elvira suppressed more laughter, then became serious. "Tell you what, Alicia, I have another friend you might like to meet, and she's far more interesting than me, I promise you. Did you never hear of *Sofonisba Anguissola*?"

"Sofo who?" I tried to make sense of the name.

"She's Italian, and she was a very, very great artist during the end of the Renaissance and almost the only woman artist of her time. She even worked with Michelangelo."

"She did?"

"Yes. It's thought that some paintings attributed to him were actually by her, or at least the sketches for them were, and she was also the official portraitist for the Spanish royal family. She painted famous portraits of King Philip and Queen Isabella and was governess to their children, whom she had the full responsibility for raising. Would you like to meet her?"

I was nearly overcome with joy. Elvira wasn't teasing. I would see her again. I looked at the earnest smiling face of my ghostly friend, at the corn-colored, mussed-up hair and blue, blue eyes, and in her country demeanor, so very English.

I barely managed to answer her. "Yes, of course, I'd love to and …"

As I spoke, I clearly heard the grating sound of a key in the lock of the church door. I turned as the door opened to see the old vicar entering.

And there was only Elvira's voice. "See you again, then."

The vicar came slowly up the aisle to me. Strangely, he didn't seem to think it odd that I was there in what was supposed to be a locked church. His age, perhaps. "Ah, good morning, young lady. You are up and about early."

"Yes, sir."

"Sketching again?"

"I was—" I hesitated. Then the words simply came out. "I—I was talking to two ghosts."

"To two ghosts?" The dear old man seemed quite unsurprised. "Were you? Yes, that's nice. There are some lovely people lying in peace around here."

"I hope you are feeling better," I said.

"Thank you, my dear. Yes, much better. Enjoy your day."

End of Part One

PART TWO

Sofonisba Anguissola

ONE

It was a month before I saw Elvira again. Dad had decided to stay on in England for a while and took us for the whole month of September to France, where the highlight for me was actually seeing the famous Bayeux Tapestry and pretending ignorance about it when I knew much more of its history than our guide or Dad or anyone else.

Finally, one crisp autumn day in October when there was frost whitening the ground every morning and when the leaves on the trees all around the old churchyard had begun to turn golden and red, covering the grass between the gravestones with a profusion of color, I saw my chance. By now, I was missing Elvira like crazy, and I got my heavy sweater and windbreaker on and biked like I'd never biked before almost wrecking myself and my bike when I ignored half-frozen pot holes. The church yard looked bleak and lonely, the church locked.

"Elvira?"

No answer.

"Elvira, please. I couldn't stand it if you started with the tease routine. I've missed you so, but I simply couldn't get here."

From somewhere there was a light musical laugh. "Excuses, excuses. The vicar's away in London town for the day and I'm inside."

I tried the huge old Church door again. It opened easily, and I found Elvira perched on the steps to the altar with her chopped-about, corn-colored hair, her blue, blue eyes, even bluer and more filled with light than ever, and her smile as devilish as always.

I had been burning to ask Elvira an important question. During the summer I had noticed flowers on many of the graves, including Elvira's, placed on special saint's days by parishioners. I decided to dive right in and ask the question now. "Elvira when we first met you said you only came from beyond to see people you wanted to see. Why did you want to see me? I can't have been the only person in four hundred years to put flowers on your grave."

"You're right. You weren't."

"But why?"

"Because you believed."

"In ghosts?"

"No. In me."

"I—I don't understand." And I didn't, not at all.

There was another silence until Elvira, suddenly

grown quite serious, said, "Alicia, when you sat down on my gravestone, you had a feeling I was there. Not just my bones or what's left of them, but 'me.' The Elvira I was when alive. And you felt it so strongly that when you brought me flowers you spoke to me from your heart as though I actually *was* alive."

She smiled then but with a smile that was different than usual. There was no mischievousness in it. "The real *you,* the Alicia you are in your heart, spoke to the real *me* I *once was,* and that made you special, and I was allowed to appear. You could try to speak to others, but unless you truly felt in your heart that you knew them, the *real* them, the way you did with me, it wouldn't work. Now do you understand?"

I still didn't, quite. But I knew I was blessed somehow and that to want more would spoil things. I said "I think so, Elvira. But what about Matilda? Why was I allowed to see her?"

"Because of me. Because I'm allowed—I can bring others."

I thought of Matilda's loving warmth and caring, for me, for someone far less than all the great people she had known and dealt with. I told Elvira how terribly sad I felt when Matilda had finally said good-bye.

"You have a friend in her," Elvira said. "She doesn't often speak of her life, and she loved telling you all about it. She wants a full report on how things go with Sofonisba because she thinks the time she lived in was a really important one in history."

I had nearly forgotten I was supposed to meet

another friend. I tried to pronounce the name and failed.

Elvira laughed. "You'll get it once you meet her." She pronounced *so-fo-nis-ba* syllable by syllable and then said, "Sofonisba Anguissola. She was born in 1535, and the next time you come here, she'll be with me. How old would you like her to be?"

"What do you mean?"

"I mean she lived to be ninety-six, and I don't think you'd get much fun out of talking to anyone that ancient." Elvira pursed her lips thoughtfully. "I think about the same age she was when she went to Florence to meet with Michelangelo. She was eighteen then, if I remember correctly."

"But Elvira, how could she suddenly be eighteen? Ghosts can change their ages just like that?"

"Of course. But only to an age within their lifetime. I couldn't change to anything older than I am right now."

That made me suddenly sad. Poor Elvira. Never to have known what it was to be a full grown woman, to have known a decent man like my father and not the brute who had always beaten her. Never to have had a happy marriage and children. She had missed so much.

I didn't have the chance to comment and probably wouldn't have. It would have perhaps been too personal and hurtful to do so. I heard the rumble of the clockworks above me in the tower and then the clang telling the half hour.

"Oh, dear! I have to get home."

"Then go. But do me a favor, okay? Next time you see the old workman raking up leaves in our churchyard, could you ask him to please set my gravestone upright again. I get teased about it all the time."

With that, she was gone.

TWO

That night I launched into all sorts of crazy brain pictures trying to imagine what this Sofonisba would look like and wondering how I'd ever talk to someone who was ninety-six, even if she looked eighteen. She wasn't a queen like Matilda, but she was a very important artist who must have been really famous. Maybe Elvira would be a tease and say she couldn't come, and then suddenly produce her the way she had Matilda.

Worst of all, what would she think of *me*? Right after I met Elvira, I rushed to the library and took out books on the Renaissance so I wouldn't look like *the* original village dropout. I learned that the Renaissance, which in French meant "rebirth," was something that happened from thirteen hundred and something to nearly sixteen hundred, when schol-ars began bringing back long-forgotten Roman and

Greek art, literature, and architecture, which caused a whole new way of thinking. Some described it as flowers suddenly appearing in a desert. At first it was mostly in Italy where it started, Wikipedia said, but later it spread to the rest of Europe, even to England. It marked the end of the Middle Ages and was a period of great art and artists and architecture, but life—I mean bathrooms and hot water and medicine and all that—still wasn't much different from when Matilda lived.

Dad helped. He came in when I was looking at a Renaissance map that showed Italy divided into a number of different countries. He said they were not really countries, they were mostly powerful cities called "city-states," and they were more or less republics. The important ones were Genoa, Naples, Milan, Florence, Sicily, and Venice. And, of course, the Vatican papal state in the middle of it all.

I asked Dad how come all this Renaissance began in Italy, and he said to take a look at where Italy was. "It's practically smack in the middle of all the major trade routes crisscrossing the Mediterranean and couldn't help but be more advanced than the northern peoples were.

"It almost didn't happen, however," Dad said. "Italy was nearly wiped out by a plague in 1350 that killed half the people in Europe."

I remembered thinking that was what Elvira had died from, until she told me she'd died in a small plague in 1588. "Was that The Black Death?"

"Yes. It was carried by fleas from rodents, rats

mostly, but of course back then they had all sorts of crazy superstitious reasons for it. Then in the sixteenth century, the French and Spanish and Austrians all decided Italy was a prize worth having, and they all invaded and fought over it like dogs. At one point the Austrians sacked Rome, and slaughtered thousands."

"Who finally won?"

"Basically the Spanish, I guess, because Spain and the Austrians, who had taken over the old German Federation of the Middle Ages, became virtually one, with the same king ruling both."

"Through inheriting them, right?"

"You knew that?"

I silently gulped. If he only knew how. I waved blithely at a book. "I've been reading that most countries were private property back then. The kings could do whatever they wanted. The people had nothing to say about it."

"Clever girl. But you know, in a funny way the Italian cities ended up the winners. Even though conquered, their, art, music, architecture, everything we call the Renaissance was a huge influence all through Europe and still is even today in America. The Renaissance wasn't just a rebirth of Italy; it was a rebirth of the entire Western world."

Getting to the churchyard, I tried to remember everything I'd read as well as what he'd told me. On the flagstone path that led between graves to the church's entry door, I felt fairly safe because I knew the vicar never came over from the vicarage on Saturdays until after lunch, which was when he wrote his sermon for Sunday.

I tapped lightly on the big oaken door. "Elvira?"

I waited and when the door didn't open, I called again. Not a sound.

"Elvira?"

This time I suddenly sensed someone and even as I did, the door suddenly swung silently open.

I began to say, "I thought you weren't coming," but stopped short. It wasn't Elvira standing there. For a moment I couldn't quite make the person out; the light in that part of the Church wasn't all that good. And then I did. I found myself looking at a smiling young woman who was an absolute killer for looks. She was not much taller than Elvira, maybe the same height as Arielle, and had tousled auburn hair that came down to below her ears and a figure that would make most movie stars eat their hearts out. She was dressed as casually as you could get in skin-fitting tights and a sort of tunic that came down mid-thighs with a broad belt around her waist and soft ankle-high boots. Almost the first thing you noticed in her face were her beautiful green eyes, which, I was to learn, revealed far more than words.

"Hello, she said. She had a soft, slightly accented voice. "You must be Alicia."

And when I could only stare because something told me this was *her*, she added, "I'm Sofonisba. I hope I didn't frighten you. Elvira wanted me to tell you that she might not be able to come today. So you'll forgive me for introducing myself in this way, won't you?" And then, as I struggled to overcome my total meltdown, she said, "Do you mind talking to me without her?"

Finally coming to my senses, I realized I could see right through her to the first line of pews, the way I could with Elvira and Matilda. I somehow managed to turn on my voice box. "Oh, no. I'm sorry. Of course not."

"Well come on in," she said, "before you freeze."

I followed her up the aisle toward the altar. As we went, she tossed out over her shoulder "Elvira said you had a terrible time pronouncing my name." She stopped to say it carefully. "It's Sofonisba Anguissola. That's a mouthful, right? My family and everybody else always just called me Sofo, and you must, too."

I murmured some inanity, and when she reached the steps to the altar and plunked herself down, I collapsed in the first pew.

"Where do you want me to start? At my beginning, maybe?" And when I was still too floored to answer, she went right on. "Sure, why not. I'm an artist. Or was. I was born in 1535, okay? And grew up in Cremona. That was a city in the north of Italy on what is called the Lombardi plain. The Italian countryside there at the foot of the Alps is mostly flat and farmland with the occasional lazy river and fields separated by lines of tall, thin poplar trees which give shade in the summer when it's very warm and break the wind off the mountains in the winter, when it can be bitterly cold. Cremona was an important center of music with a lot of churches and small palaces and a cathedral and, if you can imagine, the second highest bell tower in Italy." She broke off with a laugh. "Hometown pride." And then with a sudden concerned look she said, "Are you sure it's not too cold for you in here?"

It was, but I couldn't have cared less and managed to stammer, "No, no. Thank you. It's okay."

Sofonisba smiled. "Elvira said when the weather warms up I could sit on her gravestone, and I will."

I was still mostly speechless. Her casualness had me floored. That and the fact that she, like Elvira and Matilda, didn't seem in the least bothered by having died. They even laughed about it.

Because of Matilda I had become somewhat used to meeting famous people, but I was still nearly overwhelmed by the actual appearance of one. After all, the casual woman who now sat on the altar steps smiling warmly at me and was so absolutely gorgeous—well, she had known and worked with Michelangelo and other great artists, and she had not only lived with the King and Queen of Spain as royal portraitist but had raised the royal children.

I heard her say, "Everyone always wanted to know where I got the strange name. It was because my father was descended from Carthaginians. You know about them, don't you?"

I always feel like the original dork when first meeting anyone. But Sofo—and I already found myself thinking of her as Sofo—was different. She was so warm and friendly and laid-back, it was like I'd known her from day one. So I was beginning to recover and said I did, that in school we'd learned they were a powerful people in North Africa whose famous general, Hannibal, crossed the Mediterranean and then the Alps with a huge army, including elephants, and nearly conquered Rome.

"Great," she said. "You're dead on. And Sofonisba was a Carthaginian queen who drank poison to avoid being captured by the Romans. My father was very proud of our ancestors. Okay for all that, but now, and before I go any further, Alicia, tell me about yourself. You're American, Elvira says, and she said you draw extremely well and are already a relatively accomplished cellist. What are you doing here in England?"

I cringed a little at her knowing that I drew and stuff. After all, she was a great artist, and in comparison I was like sub-subzero. I explained about my father coming to England to do research for six months and had decided to stay longer.

Then because this new ghost in my life seemed truly interested and bombarded me with all sorts of questions about America and my family. I told her all about losing Mom and Tinker and how terrible Dad and Arielle and I had felt, and when she understood and was really sympathetic, I found myself so mellowed out that I didn't have any problems asking her about herself.

"But what about you? I mean, about your family?"

"Well, there was my father, Hamilcar—that's also a Carthaginian name. He came from a noble family in Genoa, which was a very important sea port on the western side of Italy. He was a businessman. Then there was my mother, Bianca; she'd been born a noblewoman. And then I had six sisters."

"Six?"

Sofonisba smiled at my surprise. "Six," she repeated. "And, believe it or not, we all got along quite well. I was the eldest. Then there was Elena, Lucia, Europa, Minerva, and Anna Maria. Everyone except Anna had an old Carthaginian name like me. Finally, there was my little brother, Hasdrubal. One poor male in a household of females, except for my father."

"Goodness! What size house did you have for so many?"

"A big one. It was called a *palazzo*. That's a big town house, almost a small palace, and it was in the center of Cremona on an open plaza or square near the cathedral. It was two stories high, all stone and marble. Almost all the buildings in Italy were. The Romans had cut down most of the trees that were good for building. It had a red tile roof, and downstairs there were two very big reception rooms, a dining hall, and the kitchens. A wide curved staircase led up to a balcony on the second floor where the bedrooms were. There were two of us in each one. I shared with Elena."

"How about bathrooms?"

"Oh, there weren't any. We didn't have running water. There were two privies in the back courtyard, one for the family and one for the servants, and we had chamber pots." She laughed. "I'm sure Elvira told you about them. But that's just the way things were. We didn't know anything else."

I remembered Matilda saying almost exactly the same thing. And suddenly I imagined myself a ghost telling someone in the year 2500 that having a nice warm shower was just the way things were, that we didn't know anything else, when the way those future people got clean was maybe some cyberspace magic that didn't require their taking their clothes off.

I asked what they did for a bath in Sofo's time.

"In the winter we had a metal tub in front of a fireplace where we heated water."

"That sounds like the way Queen Matilda told me she lived."

"Five hundred years before me? You're right. Having a bath hadn't changed that much. Elvira suffered the same."

I remembered very well what Matilda had told me about castles where there was no heat at all, and asked Sofonisba if her home had been heated somehow, because if it hadn't been, and since she'd said it was all stone and marble, it must have been terribly cold in the winter.

"It *was* pretty chilly, although we had four or five fireplaces where we'd burn poplar and dried-out olive wood, which filled the house with a lovely smoky odor. And my father had lined all the walls with cloth and had carpets laid on all the floors. Just the same, we had to dress very warmly, especially outdoors, where, incidentally, we were never allowed without our parents or our governess. In my day, girls in the nobility or from good families were very sheltered. We were constantly protected from men and boys with whom we weren't supposed to have anything to do until we were ready to be married, and then only with our parents or guardians present. So we girls had nobody but ourselves for company, except for our little brother, whom we all looked after and I'm afraid spoiled dreadfully. Fortunately we all got along well together. I can hardly ever remember a fight."

"Did you have anything to say about whom you married? Or were your marriages arranged?"

"Sometimes one, sometimes the other. My father, for example, never would have had any one of us marry someone we didn't want to marry. But like most parents, he tried to restrict our meeting eligible men to those he thought would be best able to take care of us. That meant how stable they were, and how much money they had, and above all, how they ranked socially. My father wouldn't think of our marrying anyone except someone from the nobility. It was often quite a different story among the higher nobility or royalty, though. A lot of women in that upper strata were married solely for political or economic reasons when love didn't come into it. And that's one reason why there were so many illicit love affairs during the Renaissance. Even though the church was everywhere, people were far less frightened of it, and there was much less religious restriction than in Matilda's day. It wasn't a sin to fall in love, and people cheated a lot." She laughed. "Or claimed they were in love so they could misbehave as they pleased."

The ghostly artist paused then, and said, "But to get back to my life. In the summer, everything was quite different. Our Cremona house was wonderfully cool then, but the streets were boiling hot, and the stench from them wasn't very pleasant. The town was terribly slow about cleaning up after all the animals, the dogs and cats and of course the horses and donkeys and oxen. When it rained the streets were not very attractive and always crowded with carts and people.

"Our courtyard was hardly big enough for any sort of outdoor activity, so every May we'd all pile into a horse-drawn carriage and flee down the dusty road between Cremona and Milan to our country home, an hour away. We'd stay there for the whole summer, right up until October. We were quite well-off and had a large house with an extensive property around it that gave us plenty of space to play in or just to walk about on. It was by a lovely river that we bathed in and that had tall poplar trees all along its banks. There was one deep pool we could dive into. We didn't have bathing suits, and no girl then would ever dream of swimming naked, so we would simply take off our dresses and run around and swim in our underwear, which was usually cotton or silk camisoles and pantaloons that came down to our ankles. None of the male employees or even any of the farmers around there were allowed anywhere near our swimming place. My father was often away on business—he had a lot of political connections—and my mother was not very well, but our governess was very strict, and everyone around our country home was afraid of her, except us. We were all very fond of her. Even more than our father, she was the one who taught us to read and write. Then there was a cook and several servants. Our food in the summer was better than in town because we had a lovely, big vegetable garden, and everything we ate was fresh. We almost always dined outdoors. There was a huge carob tree on our front terrace that gave wonderful shade and had a large table under it. And we'd also sit there to read and use the table for everything besides eating. Under that wonderful old tree was when I started, around age four or five, to sketch things."

"And then you became very famous."

Sofonisba laughed. "Yes, I did become famous, but only after a lot of really hard work for what seemed like forever. Perhaps in the different world today, where there is television and photography and instant communication, I might have been something else. But in Italy back then there was none of that. Painting was our only way of seeing ourselves, of preserving who we were and how we lived, and expressing our thoughts. And art and artists were everywhere. It was strictly a man's world, though, so it wasn't easy for me. Women in my day didn't work or have careers. They married and were wives and raised children. They were trained for that, and to marry into nobility, they also had to be proficient in writing, music, embroidery, languages, and the arts."

"That also sounds just like in Matilda's day."

"Queen Matilda again? You're right. Things for women hadn't changed that much. My father, however, was particularly interested in our painting well because he loved paintings. He knew a number of famous artists, and he had a commission to search for the right one to do the frescoes in several important cathedrals and public buildings. So that's how I got started."

"But how did you learn? I mean, in America we have art classes."

"I'm afraid we didn't have those. When it came to art, my father dropped everything and taught us some of the most basic things he'd had to learn himself as a child along with anything he'd picked up since. Mostly, he showed us how to cut chalk and draw."

"What do you mean, cut chalk?"

Sofo stared blankly a moment as though she didn't understand, and then looked aware. "Oh, I understand. You can buy your art supplies: chalk and crayons and paint and all that. We had to make ours ourselves. Chalk was either white or red or brown, sometimes black. It was cut out of chalk deposits in the mountains, and we learned to whittle pieces into shape like a crayon with a sharp point, or a dull one, depending on what you wanted to sketch. Sketching was very important because all painting was done over something drawn first, a person or a landscape or whatever."

"What about the paint?" I tried to imagine what sort of tubes they had because I was sure they couldn't be like ours.

"We made our own."

"Paint, too? You did? Cool. How?"

"You mixed your different colors of pigment with oil, either linseed or walnut—I liked walnut best—and then you did what you do today. You'd mix the different colors together, blues, yellows, whites, green, red, to get the exact color you wanted. That was the easy part. The hard part was the pigment. Some of it came from vegetation, even from earth, but most of it came from rocks."

"Rocks?"

Sofonisba nodded. "Rocks. The blue, for example, often came from extremely expensive lapis lazuli, the green from tourmaline. The rock had to be to be ground up by hand with a brass mortar and pestle." She held up her hands. "I had wrists like iron because of it. Later, when I was older, and especially when I worked in Spain, a lot of the pigment came ready-ground from North Africa or the Orient."

"But then once you had paint, who taught you how actually to paint something?"

Sofonisba was thoughtful a moment, remembering. Then she said, "You know, life often turns out to be a certain way because somewhere at the beginning you are lucky, or fate steps in. Who knows? With me, that happened when I was just seven. I had done a drawing in red chalk on a bit of parchment. It was a rather naughty sketch of our governess looking like a devil with a tail and horns." She paused, smiling to herself at the memory, and then said "I'd thrown it out, and a maid collecting the trash saw it. She was laughing her head off, because she didn't like the governess, when my father came by and saw it. I thought I was really going to be in trouble, but instead he studied it carefully, and decided I had real talent and, since he had connections, he arranged for me to take lessons from an established painter in Cremona. This was a well-known artist named Bernardino Campi."

"And you were only seven?" I couldn't imagine anyone being interested in the scrawls I had made when I was that age.

"I know that seems terribly young," Sofo agreed, "and I suppose it was, but remember I had started off when I was only three or four. It was a little unfair that I was the one picked for formal lessons because my sisters were just as good as I was, especially the next one to me, Elena. I tried to make up for it by teaching them everything I picked up from Bernardino. And it was in those years that I really learned painting. Bernardino said "If you want to learn, you have to create paint. That means not just the paint itself but what you paint *with*—your brushes—as well as what you paint on—wood or canvas." And he was one tough guy. Nothing pleased him except "perfect," and my being only a little girl didn't count. It was "Do it or else." He used to carry a switch, and he made me do everything from the bottom up and do it right, or *swish*, right across my hands."

"Gosh! He did that? Really?"

"Of course, and better than the blows I understand poor Elvira suffered. People weren't easy on children back then. You shaped up or else. Bernardino also made me prepare smooth wood with a special glaze, for him as well as for me, and to stretch linen or canvas onto wooden frames and tighten them with a coat of glue. For years, I ground all his pigments as well as my own, and made brushes. Oh, the brushes, they went on forever."

"How did you do them?"

"We whittled hardwood for handles—oak was best, or chestnut. We'd then prepare the bristles, which would be of badger or horse hair. I'd cluster them or splay them flat and either tie them onto the end of the handle with fishnet twine saturated with glue, or I'd strap them on with narrow strips of zinc or brass. When I got good enough at all of that, Bernardino had me mix paint and then put first coats onto drawings to provide a base for finishing a work. For years, almost my whole childhood, I practically lived in his workshop."

"But did you get any painting done yourself?"

"Oh, yes, and once I started actually to paint, he was wonderfully helpful. He was a dry sort of man who didn't talk much, but he was marvelous at showing how. I should paint things by painting them myself. Then, when I was about ten, my sister Anna Maria died."

"The plague?"

"No. Nobody knew why. She caught a cold and then ran a high fever, and the next thing we knew, she was dead. It was awful. The whole house was draped in black for weeks. Too soon afterward, my mother also died. She'd been sick a long time, and suddenly one day she wasn't there any longer. My poor father—it was terrible for him. We girls all tried to put our own sadness to one side and cheer him up as much as possible. I painted endless silly cartoons to bring a smile to his tired old face. Elena made up crazy tunes on the piano with even crazier lyrics. Europa and Minerva and Lucia formed a singing group. And then Lucia died, too, again of some awful disease that nobody knew anything about."

"Oh, no," I exclaimed.

"It was beyond awful," Sofo said. "One day she was fine, and a week later we were burying her. I always thought she was the best artist of all of us and would have made me look silly had she lived. Death, I'm afraid, was very much part of life in those days. It was everywhere and all the time. Our medicine was no better than Matilda's. It was either some awful mix of foul herbs or whatever, or you were bled, which, of course, you moderns know was probably the worst thing to do.

"Meanwhile as I grew up I became quite good. Bernardino Campi once told me I was every bit as good as he; I remember he sort of growled it out of the corner of his mouth. I didn't believe him, but just the same I gave presents of portraits to friends everywhere, and people began to know me and take me seriously as an artist. I was severely restricted to just portraits, however."

"Oh? Why was that?"

"It was because women of my class in my day weren't allowed to see the naked human body. Hence

I couldn't study anatomy, either from live models or corpses."

"You couldn't even see other women?"

"No. And that kind of ignorance kept me from doing the sort of grand religious paintings involving numbers of people, the most popular form of art then. In those, you had to position people's bodies in all sorts of different positions, and you needed to really understand anatomy to do that. Nobody really wanted portraits. They simply ordered them to have a record of their existence because there was no other way. And small wonder, because portraits in those days were very stiff and rigidly formal. They made a person look absolutely wooden. I found a way around that, however. I decided to paint people in more relaxed family settings, and did one of myself and two of my sisters playing chess with our governess watching us. It drew immediate attention. A girl painted this? I was just fourteen, and people couldn't believe it."

"Wow! That's fabulous."

"It was more than fabulous, Alicia. It was really quite daring. Women artists were virtually unheard of then. About this time, I painted what became one of my most well-known early self-portraits. I painted Bernardino Campi painting *me*. It was again a whole different slant on portrait painting, and it created quite a stir. It brought me to the attention of a number of important people around Cremona, but not the ones who really counted."

"But who did, then?"

"Ah, good question. Cremona was an agricultural and business center. It didn't really count for much in the art world. Florence and Rome were where everything was happening, where all the truly great artists were and all the great works were being done, and of course, nobody there had ever heard of me. Remember, communications weren't what they are today, and Italy was broken up into different states that more often than not weren't speaking to each other. In fact, if they weren't fighting with words, they would actually be at war. And then, of course, since everyone wanted Italy's wealth, Italy was constantly being invaded and fought over by the French and the Spanish, the Austrians, and even the English. The north of Italy was under Spanish rule when I grew up.

"About this time, Bernardino Campi moved to another city, and I was left without an instructor until my father persuaded another well-known artist, Bernardino Gatti, to take me on. I didn't like him as much as Bernardino Campi, who, rough as he was, I had grown to adore. In fact, I really didn't like Gatti at all. He was often thoroughly unpleasant to deal with, and in order to put me down whenever there was a dispute, he'd remind me that he'd been an apprentice to the great Correggio.

"I didn't learn much from him either. What I really needed wasn't more instruction but to get out of being just the local girl who made good. Again, luck or fate, although mostly my dear father, stepped in. He had wholly accepted that I would be an artist in life and not a demure housewife, and he proudly made sure everyone knew about me and my talent in the various Spanish courts he did business with. This got me a commission to paint the Spanish duchess Margherita and her daughter in law, Elena of Austria. When the portraits drew a great deal of attention, I persuaded my father to let me go to Rome."

"At which point I am going to persuade Alicia to come home for lunch and stop talking to herself in an empty church."

The voice from right behind me came as a shock. For an instant I thought I'd been discovered by Arielle. I spun around and there, rippling with laughter, was Elvira, imitating my sister. She flitted past me to land abruptly on the altar steps beside Sofonisba, leaving me to slowly get over my surprise and not knowing whether to scold her for frightening me or to join in her laughter.

"If you have a date, then this is a good time to take a break in my story," Sofo said. "Anyway, I'm sure you have had enough of me learning how to make and mix paint."

"No, I haven't," I protested.

Then Sofo stood up. "But I do have to go. I've loved talking to you, and the next time we meet, I'll tell you how I got to meet Michelangelo and work with him. And what it was like living in Florence and Rome before America was discovered."

"I'll bet she'll want to hear about your romances," Elvira said.

"And why not?" Sofo replied. "In my time romance was almost more important than breathing. And I know. I spent most of my youth falling in love."

With that, she promptly disappeared.

"Oh, Elvira," I said. "She's just wonderful."

"I told you so." Elvira suddenly looked contrite. "Alicia, I'm sorry. Will you forgive me for teasing you?"

I saw by the seriousness in Elvira's usually dancing eyes that she meant it, and my heart flipped a little. I forgot sometimes how very dear Elvira was and how important. If it wasn't for her, I wouldn't have met Queen Matilda, nor Sofonisba.

"Will you come next time with Sofo?"

"If you want me to."

"I think I'd die if you didn't."

A slow smile broke over Elvira's face. "Oh, what a lovely idea. Then you'd be a ghost too, and we could go together all over eternity scaring people out of their wits."

She blew me a kiss and disappeared as suddenly as Sofonisba had.

THREE

There were times when I felt I simply had to tell someone about my ghostly friends, but I didn't. They would have to be my secret and nobody else's. Others simply weren't on the same wavelength as me.

"You just never know with people," Sofo said when I confessed to having sent up a trial balloon. I had barely mentioned ghosts to Arielle, who had laughed and said, "Don't be stupid. Ghosts don't exist. They're only in people's imaginations."

"Some take it as completely natural that they're seeing a ghost," Sofo said. "It's as though they saw one every day. And then others are so scared they think their last moment on earth has arrived. I always feel terrible when by mistake someone sees me and shrieks and runs away."

It was afternoon, and I'd come by the churchyard

on my way back from the library in Henley. The sun was still up and warming the world, so we met outside by Elvira's grave, now covered with fallen autumn leaves.

"But scaring people is half the fun," Elvira said.

Sofo gave her a long "shut up and behave" look, Elvira pretended contrition, and with that, Sofo got right into her story.

"After four years of Gatti," she said, "besides being fed up with forever being his student when actually I had begun painting far better than he, I really felt the need to spread my wings. That, as I told you, meant Rome and the papacy and Florence, all three teeming with the wealth of the famous and powerful Medici family. Their leader, Cosimo, adored painting, and he showered the world of art with gold to promote it. So I headed first for Rome."

"Cool! All by yourself?"

"Yes."

"What did your father say?"

"I was only eighteen, and I guess he could have stopped me. Young women in Italy back then didn't go anywhere without being escorted. But to my surprise, he not only didn't object but urged me to. He gave me money to get started and letters of introduction to various highly placed people he knew. Even better, he sent a couple of my paintings to people close to the pope—that was Julius III at that time—who was a big supporter of artists. One of his friends was the great Giorgio Vasari, whom he'd come to know well and who had once visited us at home and encouraged us all, especially me, to keep up our painting."

"Who was he?"

"Vasari? He was an important painter but an even more important architect, and was most famous as an art critic. He wrote a book dedicated to Cosimo de Medici called *Lives*—biographies of all the important painters of the time. Vasari originated the word *Renaissance* and used it to describe the explosive rebirth of art everywhere after it had been half-dead for centuries. In his book he also examined the many different techniques of painting and the materials used."

"You were lucky to have a father like yours," Elvira said.

I heard sadness in her tone and remembered when talking to Matilda how Elvira always felt slightly inferior to other people, which, I had begun to realize, was the true reason for all her teasing and mischievousness. "My father did nothing," she continued, "but plow fields and sow corn. He couldn't even read or write."

Sofo put an arm around Elvira's shoulder and drew her close. "Nonsense, Elvira. The world can't live without people providing them with food, even your beastly father. There are more important things in the world than reading and writing."

"I guess," Elvira said, and I could see how grateful she was for the kind words.

"Where did you live in Rome?" I asked. "I mean, without a family."

I stayed at the home of the dowager duchess

Domato, who took me in as a favor to the Duchess Margherita."

"The one whose portrait you painted? What was she like?"

Sofo broke into a laugh. "The duchess Domato? She was a dried up old prune who had a fit every time I went out in the street by myself. She thought any woman alone in Rome was nothing more than a harlot. And in a way I suppose she was right to think so, for the streets swarmed with prostitutes along with every other kind of riffraff: peddlers of stolen merchandize, con artists, pickpockets, and ruthless monsters who would as soon run a knife through you for your purse as take a deep breath. Worse than any of them were the nobility dandies all dressed in the latest fashion, their hair curled and perfumed, a sword or dagger at their hip, and looking to seduce some poor innocent girl." Sofo rolled her eyes despairingly. "They were so persistent, and vanity in men is so, so *boring*."

"There were no police?"

"Not really. There were small bands of watchmen, usually privately paid by some great title like Cosimo de Medici, who had a small army of them. The streets were narrow and paved, there were no sidewalks, and at night they were almost pitch dark and lit only by the occasional resin torch held aloft on a wall bracket. I most certainly stayed off them, although once or twice I tarried too long and got caught out. It was scary."

"I think most of them in London Town were like that, too." Elvira said. "I had a friend who one time went up there. She said she spent her whole time knocking off hands and slapping faces and kicking shins."

"What did you do, Sofo?" I asked. By now, I had become quite used to calling the great artist by her nickname.

"I took my father's advice. Dress like a lady, walk like a lady, head high, speak like a lady, and keep your eyes straight ahead and ignore any man who speaks or even looks at you. It worked. I was almost never bothered."

"When did you meet Michelangelo?"

"Not for quite a while. At first, not knowing any-one, I simply wandered about Rome and did a lot of sketching and observing. Using my father's introduc-tions, I met a few artists, and perhaps more impor-tantly, patrons of the arts."

Elvira suddenly had a question. "Sofo. Wait. What happened to the art critic? Was his name Vasari?"

"Right. Georgio Vasari. Well, I had started to wonder that myself when one morning, shortly after breakfast, old prune-face's maid interrupted a sketch I was doing to tell me there was a gentleman at the door who wanted to see me. I figured I was safe enough in the duchess's home and went to the door. And guess who it was?"

"Vasari, of course," I exclaimed.

"None other. He had a couple of sketches my father had sent him and one portrait, and he wanted to know if it was really I who had done the work." She laughed. "He couldn't believe any woman could do such a thing. To prove it, I showed him the sketch I was working on, which was of a girl laughing with joy over the antics of a kitten. And I'll never forget what he said. "With your kind permission, Sofonisba, I would like to borrow this sketch to show to my old friend Michelangelo."

"Well, as you can imagine, I can't remember anything of what we talked about after that until he bowed and left, taking my sketch with him."

Elvira was unable to resist giving Sofonisba a hug. "Don't stop. Tell us. What did Michelangelo say? About the sketch, I mean. And how long did you have to wait to meet him?"

"His answer came back quite soon and was delivered again and in person by Georgio. "The master," he said, "would like to see your rendition of the opposite emotion to your laughing girl sketch."

"Crying?" I asked.

"Well yes," Sofo said, "but I realized right away that that could be almost anything. I thought hard on it for a day or so. Artists then, if not painting portraits, were painting religious scenes. They either depicted famous legends or myths involving the Greek gods, or they painted great moments in the Bible like the Crucifixion or the Virgin Mother with Jesus as a baby. I said to myself, Michelangelo is the man who sculpted the magnificent *Pieta*—The Virgin mother holding the crucified Christ in her lap. I knew that no weeping Madonna I could sketch could ever come close to that, so I decided not to even try. I needed to go a whole different route.

"For several days I was miserable with frustration. I couldn't think of anything. Then I took a chance at something that suddenly popped into my head. I sketched a little boy crying when a crayfish in a tray full of them, held by a smiling girl, bit his finger. And held my breath. It was a crazy chance to take. It was so far removed from any sort of the usual work with a religious emphasis. I didn't dare give it to Vasari because I was sure he would never have given it to Michelangelo. So I wrapped it up and sent it to where I knew Michelangelo had his studio."

"And? What happened? What did he say?" Elvira and I both asked at once.

'I waited for almost a week. And when I heard from neither Vasari nor the master, I put on my best dress and shoes and went to Michelangelo's studio myself. It was at the end of a narrow cobbled street where the houses, which were very old and almost leaning against each other, nearly shut out the sun but which opened onto a lovely little square or plaza where there was a fountain. His studio was a house at one side of it with two big double doors. It was a warm day, the doors were open, so I just walked in. I found myself in a huge room where three apprentices were working away on making some canvasses ready for painting over sketches, which I could tell at once were done by the master. Birds were fluttering about in the rafters high overhead, and there were two unfinished statues appearing halfway out of huge blocks of marble. I say 'appearing' because I was to learn that Michelangelo felt that statues were already in blocks of stone and only needed to be brought out by chiseling away the stone that hid them.

"The place was work, work, work, and I was completely intimidated. I summoned up my courage and asked for the master, and someone pointed to the door of an adjoining room. I went to it, knocked. No answer. I pushed the door open and found myself in a terribly untidy place in which there was a table with the remains of a small meal, a slice of meat and a potato, and there was a chair and an unmade narrow bed. That was all. It was dark compared to the brightness of the studio, and it was a moment before I saw my sketch of the little boy crying. It was all by itself on an easel.

I had gone to look at it when I heard a rough voice say, "You drew that, did you?" And the master appeared out of a sort of open closet where some appallingly shabby clothes were hanging. I couldn't believe the man who spoke and approached me was actually Michelangelo, but I knew he was because, of course, I had seen portraits and sketches of him. His clothes looked as though they hadn't been cleaned in a month, his hair and beard were an uncombed tangle, and he smelled of onions. He looked tired and haggard, too, and he was older than I expected. I knew at once he had to be close to eighty. I started to confess that I was guilty of the sketch when he abruptly interrupted.

"Go in there and get busy." He waved at the adjacent work room. He grabbed a handful of sketches that were lying scattered on the floor and shoved them at me. "Redo these in your own style, and when you come tomorrow, come dressed for work."

"With that, he shuffled off back to the dark closet. My interview was clearly over. I left, walking on air."

"But he said nothing else? Just that?" I asked.

"Not a word."

"And he was like that, really? This famous man and with all his great wealth?" Elvira wondered. "Like some homeless person?"

Sofo nodded. "He was like that. And for all the time I spent with him, he rarely spoke to me; he rarely even smiled. Actually that was true of his way with everyone, not just me. But for all his abrupt gruffness, he was enormously kind. It's just that he was so deep into his creations that the world didn't really exist for him. He was unaware of anything but creation, and because of his genius he was accepted everywhere, no matter how he looked."

"How did he help your work?"

"By making me work. Morning noon and night, it seemed. He had me improve on a lot of his sketches before he painted over them, and sometimes had me paint over them myself. He also had me paint stuff of my own, and endlessly. More important, perhaps, he spoke a lot about me to others and introduced me to people. He took me off many times to the Vatican where he was designing the great dome of St. Peter's. We must have made an odd pair. I remember a lot of heads turned as we walked down streets—a rough unkempt old man in his eighties and a young woman barely in her twenties in her finest dress. On the second one of those visits, he introduced me to the pope."

"You met the pope?"

"Yes, indeed. He commissioned me to do some portraits of members of his family and one of his favorite cardinals, and besides paying me more than handsomely, he gave me some wonderful and very valuable jewelry."

"Awesome! Was jewelry big then in Italy?"

"Huge. Just the way fashion was. It changed constantly, and one of the marks of one's social position was how well one dressed. In the Renaissance we dressed beautifully. Largely because of that I became fascinated by painting the silk and lace on the clothes of many of the women. It took hours and hours, but I never got tired of it, and it gave a special kind or reality to a portrait. Besides their clothes, women back then spent more time on makeup and personal cosmetics than they do now. In fact, from my point of view, they were obsessed with it."

"Does that mean you didn't?"

"I didn't care about all that fashion stuff. I was totally sunk in my painting. I soon abandoned fancy dressing and went around in my work clothes or otherwise dressed modestly. My father and Vasari both said *too* modestly, because there I was, all of a sudden quite famous. I couldn't believe it. And famous not just with the rich, who clamored for my portraits of them and made me suddenly rich also, but as an artist among other artists. I began to have copiers, can you imagine? Leading artists copied the style I had created—portraits that had life going on around them."

Sofo shook her head at a sudden memory. "I remember waking up one morning after an evening of incredible compliments by Francesco Salviati, a well-known painter, and the poet Angelo Grillo, and saying to myself, "Was that really me they were talking about?"

"What I want to hear about most," Elvira said with a devilish smile that even the darkness of the churchyard night couldn't hide, "was what you had for love affairs."

Sofo laughed. "Elvira you really are … what was the word again, Alicia?"

"Incorrigible," I said.

"Exactly. Affairs, the way I bet you are thinking of them, you little devil, didn't exist for well brought-up young women. Until married, we were abstinence and chastity personified. But that's not to say," she added to mollify Elvira's slightly chastened look, "that I didn't give my heart to a few young gallants. Or flirt wickedly. We Italians were romantic beyond all reason. Everything in our lives—food, clothing, music, art, even our manners—created an atmosphere of romance, and falling in love was everywhere with everyone. I can well remember being so in love that I could hardly eat or sleep."

"Compared to England at the same time, I always heard that Italy was like heaven," Elvira said.

"Is that true?" I asked Sofo.

"Yes. Elvira is right. We were so very alive. We

threw away a lot of medieval rules and embraced life, while at the same time we were quite proper, especially when it came to manners. Everyone's personal comportment was very important: how you spoke to people or wrote, all that, and most of all, what you wore. Fashion for both men and women was everything. We were more educated, too, in many ways. We were the most advanced in music in Europe. There was music everywhere. In all the homes and in the streets, too, you heard mandolins, guitars, flutes. It filled our lives with sound. In those days a lot of communication was also by letters. We wrote them endlessly, and we read more. Printing had been invented, and in Italy small printers turned out books endlessly, which were gobbled up by everyone."

I remembered, as Sofo spoke, that I'd heard about their music from my father, who was a classical music enthusiast like me. He said that the Italians had virtually invented the keyboard and thus the piano, and had also invented the violin, and that their favorite form of music outside of choral arrangements for churches was the madrigal, which spread all over Europe. He also said that many of the greatest operas were written by Italians, and usually with a romantic theme.

I could hardly believe I was sitting talking to a young woman who had lived all that, but I wanted to get back to painting. I said, "Could you tell us about the Duke of Alba and what happened?" I had read about him in the Henley library.

"Ah, yes. The Duke. Well, I'd gone to Florence where I was introduced to its leader, the great Cosimo de Medici, who was perhaps Italy's most formidable patron of art, even more so than the pope. I guess I'd been there about two years and had painted a lot of portraits and met a lot of other artists, some very established. Quite a few, even some of the greats, were already copying my style of portraits, the way I departed from the old, very rigid way of doing them. More importantly, I was able to connect with several other women artists and compare notes with them. There weren't many. There was the Flemish painter Lavinia Teerlinc, who was visiting, and there was a very gifted woman from Bologna named Lavinia Fontana. There was also Artemisia Gentileschi in Rome. They were excellent on their own, and the most I could do was to encourage them not to be put down by many of the men who found women in the arts a joke. If and when they gave credit at all, they gave it to the women's teachers.

"Then one day I had just finished a portrait with the moon showing through the window of the room where the subject was reading by candlelight when dear old Giorgio Vasari came by. He was there to supervise work on the famous arcade bridge over the River Arno and the grand loggia entrance to the Uffizi Palace that he had designed. He insisted I go with him to Milan, still under Spanish rule, to meet the Duke of Alba and also the Duca di Sessa of the Spanish court, who at the time was the governor there and who had heard of me because he was a patron of Bernardino Campi, my first teacher. That was in 1558, and I was just twenty-three."

"And world-famous already," exclaimed Elvira.

"Well, not quite 'world.'"

"As good as," cried Elvira, and didn't stop there. "By then, everyone knew of you all over Europe. You'd done portraits of everyone who counted, and what they didn't say about you, your father and Vasari did. So don't be so modest."

When Sofo surrendered with a warm smile, I asked, "Did you end up painting the Duke's portrait?"

"I did. And the portraits of several of his friends. And I guess that was a huge turning point in my painting life. I had hardly returned to Florence when I was visited by the Duke of Sessa as personal emissary from the King of Spain. At the time that was King Philip, and he'd been sent several paintings of mine by the Duke of Alba. I was invited to come to Spain to paint portraits of the royal family and to teach the royal princesses to paint as well. I was to be given not only a very substantial income for my services but an official position as lady-in-waiting to the new French-born queen, Elisabeth of Valois, who in Spain was called Isabella."

That was all I heard from Sofo that day. It was all of a sudden getting quite dark and, with the sun gone down, very chilly. After all, winter had almost arrived.

Bicycling home, I didn't see any of the half-frozen Thames Valley. In my mind I was walking with Sofo through the crowded streets of Florence and Rome, looking up at the flower boxes that seemed to spring from every window of the ancient brick buildings so crammed against each other, hearing all the sounds and seeing the endless statuary that decorated every square, and filling my heart with the endless music that was constantly in the streets back then.

FOUR

We next met inside the church because there'd been a dusting of snow during the night and it was chilly.

Sofo sat on the altar steps next to Elvira and picked right up on her story, as though there had never been any interruption. "I don't know if I was more flattered," she said, "at what was being offered me or by King Phillip's sending such an important person to tell me. Just the same, I hesitated. It was a huge commitment, and I wasn't sure I could bear being taken away from my Italian life or from the remains of my family in Cremona. With no magazines or newspapers or television, there was no way to know what Spain was like. It would be the same as going to America the way a few courageous adventurers were beginning to do. I'd be completely on my own.

"There was no back and forth-ing between Spain

and Italy. Travel in my time was dangerous, and it took forever to get from one part of Europe to another. A million questions filled my mind, and it was hard for me to sleep at night. Would the court be like ours, or even more formal? What would the countryside look like? And the towns? And the Spanish language? Would I be expected to speak it?—I didn't know a word. Or did the nobility speak French the way so many of our nobility did, especially since their new queen was French? And what would the children be like—had they already learned anything about art? And, of course, above all—what would the King and Queen think of me?

"I hesitated. Then something happened that made up my mind for me. My sister Elena, whom I adored and always thought was as good if not a better artist than I, took vows and entered a convent. That made her virtually lost to me forever."

"Oh, misery," I said. I remembered that convent business from talking to Matilda—the hard, lost lives of nuns cut off forever from real life and from all their family and friends. I instantly felt sad for Sofo, and asked about her father.

"My father? The poor old dear had his hands full with the education of my younger brother, Hasdrubal, who was following his footsteps in his business. When my father came to Genoa to say good-bye to me, I knew I'd never see him again, this wonderful, wonderful man who had so believed in me that he had broken all the rules about how young women should behave and what their lives should be and had sent me off into the world to be an artist. The farewell nearly broke my heart. I almost didn't go, and I cried for days after. But he insisted, and I knew I would be foolish not to. Other than him, there was no reason to stay. My sister Europa was successfully married, and Minerva had turned writer and scholar, her life filled with the university where she was already a professor."

I tried to imagine parting from my own father forever and felt some of the pain I was sure Sofonisba had suffered. "Just the same," I said, "it was awfully brave of you. What was the trip like?"

"It was beyond my wildest dreams. I went first by sea to avoid the long overland trip across the south of France, which was still hostile to Spain. The sea voyage was dangerous, too. Storms in the Mediterranean can be sudden and very violent. But the trip was nothing in excitement compared to what the King had prepared for me. To ensure my safety, King Phillip had ordered one of his largest naval vessels specially outfitted just for me. I had a whole sort of royal suite to myself. If that wasn't overwhelming enough and a complete surprise, I had an escort of two noblewomen as maids-of-honor, two gentlemen chamberlains, and six servants who were all in livery. For me? Sofonisba Anguissola? A girl from Cremona?"

"Awesome! You must have just about flipped."

"I most certainly did. And wait, there was more. I also had an armed guard of a dozen handpicked soldiers whose captain was one of the handsomest men I had ever seen. I did three sketches of him on the voyage for him to give to his mother.

"It gave me quite a shock at the dock in Genoa when I first was presented to such an incredible entourage. Surely I hardly merited any of it. I was just one more Italian artist, even though a successful one, and even though writers and artists were highly respected back then and were almost always granted special privileges. I really had to wonder what lay ahead for me in Spain. Well, we got there and, yes, my escort was just the beginning. Guess who greeted me at the dock as though I were the King of England arriving? None other than King Phillip himself."

"You're kidding."

"I'm not. And he'd brought his queen, Elisabeth of Valois, whose name in Spanish was Isabella. Can you imagine?"

"Far out. What did you do?"

"I think that's where all my father's training for his daughters to conduct themselves like noble-women came in. I somehow managed to behave as though I were quite used to that sort of thing."

"La-di-da," Elvira exclaimed and rose to flounce about the altar, making both Sofo and me laugh.

"The King's beautiful manners helped," Sofo continued, "but I think what really made it possible for me was his wife. Queen Isabella was my age, and we became close friends on first sight. It was as though she wasn't royalty at all. When I painted her portrait later, my whole heart went into it, and what you see in that picture was exactly what she was like, the loveliest person imaginable.

"It took almost a week to get to the new royal palace in Madrid. Remember, there were virtually no roads then. The royal party, me included, went in very ornate carriages, and the ride was rough. We were constantly jostled about like corks bobbing in a rushing stream. When we finally arrived, I could hardly believe the size of the palace. It was absolutely huge. It had two thousand eight hundred rooms, can you imagine? It was several stories high, and it sat across the entire end of a vast paved parade ground which was flanked on each side by long loggias. It was called the Palacio de Oriente, the Palace of the Far East."

"Far East?" I asked. "Why was that?"

Sofo explained. "Not the Far East you would think of, China perhaps. It only meant it was very east of where the royal palace had always been in Valladolid. That was another Spanish city, more in the center of Spain and considerably west of Madrid. King Phillip had ordered the construction of the new palace twenty-five years before and had only just moved in, so it was brand new. And since Spain was plundering newly discovered South America of its riches, it was incredibly ornate. Everything was marble and gold. I was escorted by two of Queen Isabella's ladies to a suite of rooms that would be my home for the next fourteen years. The suite was in the same wing as the queen's apartments and had every comfort you could imagine, including a lovely view from a terrace out over gardens with grassy lawns, and little paths among fruit trees, and a beautiful fountain. There were four rooms altogether: the bedroom with a fireplace and a big four-poster bed, a gilded settee and chairs, and ornate wardrobes to keep clothes in. There was a private bathroom with a large round porcelain tub and a marble toilet over a shaft that went who knows where. Above a large decorated porcelain bowl for washing, there was a big tank with a spigot that was filled with fresh water every day from somewhere above my suite. There was a delightfully cozy small room, also with a fireplace, some shelves for books, and a writing desk with a leather top. Finally and next to all that, there was a studio where I would paint. This was a large bare room with a worktable and an easel, a wide-plank wooden floor of polished oak, and a tall floor-to-ceiling window with north light. I was once again overwhelmed. All I could think of was that I would suffer the most acute embarrassment if I failed to turn out paintings that would justify all this."

"How soon did you have to start to work?"

"Oh, not immediately. I had to be introduced to the court first as well as get settled. Queen Isabella was wonderfully helpful and took me everywhere herself. You see, she had only been married to the king for two years when I arrived, so a lot of it was still new to her. She was his third wife."

"His third?" I couldn't imagine anyone being married three times. "What happened to the first two?"

"The first one was his cousin, Maria of Portugal. She died bringing a son, Carlos, into the world."

"She was his cousin?"

"There were a lot of inter-family marriages back then. Three of King Phillip's wives were his nieces."

"But that's awful."

"Yes, but don't forget that marriage was still a political or economic arrangement, just as in Matilda's day in the Middle Ages. The fact that a man was marrying a niece or cousin was simply ignored."

"Did brothers and sisters marry?"

"No. They drew the line there, thank heaven."

"Who was his second wife?"

"His second wife was Queen Mary of England, another cousin, and that was strictly a political alliance. European kingdoms then were still pretty much owned by their monarchs and treated like private properties. Mary needed Spain as a bulwark against France and the Hapsburg Empire, which had evolved from the German Federation of Matilda's day. Philip needed England off his back when it came to the Netherlands, which he had inherited. So, for a short while, he was the English King as well as the Spanish one. But it only lasted four years until she died. They had no children."

It seemed a terrible jumble to me, and I suddenly felt sorry for Queen Isabella. "With all those wives, what was *he* like?"

"King Phillip? He was two people, really. One was a man hated by many as a ruthless and cruel despot. All Europe at that time was half torn apart by Protestantism with its beginnings under Martin Luther, the priest who had challenged the corruption of the Church in Rome and the venality of its popes. Philip, who was devoutly Catholic, saw Protestantism as the worst possible heresy. Under him the infamous

Inquisition in Spain was created. It consisted of special courts that sought to prove whether someone was secretly Protestant, usually by the most terrible torture, and thousands of Protestants were burned at the stake."

"Spain was mostly Catholic?"

"Yes, as were France and Italy. Much of the north of Europe embraced Protestantism, however, and Catholics were killing Protestants, and Protestants were killing Catholics in a virtual blood bath. For example; Phillip, who was dedicated to the complete destruction of any religion that wasn't Catholic, spent years fighting the Netherlands, which had become almost totally Protestant. Thousands died."

"In England, Queen Elizabeth was secretly Protestant, while more or less pretending she was still Catholic," Elvira said.

"Shrewd politics," Sofo said. "It probably saved a lot of lives. Spanish court life was removed from any discord, however, and I saw in King Phillip a completely different person. I saw an elegant and gracious man, a loving and devoted husband and father who was warm and kind to those who served him. He was hard working, too. He was endlessly active in the business of ruling. He also had his hands full holding back the Turks, who wanted all the prizes of the West, especially Italy, and there was endless trouble with the major provinces of Spain still trying to cling to laws and customs they had enjoyed until unified by his father. Finally, not even all the vast riches from Spain's conquest of Mexico and South America—the ships were constantly arriving loaded with gold—could settle the huge debt his father had run up."

"He took quite a licking from us," Elvira put in, with sudden pride. "We smashed to pieces the huge armada he sent to conquer England."

"Helped by a hurricane," Sofo said tartly. "His armada was one reason why the English hated him so. All their history about him is colored by that."

I sensed an argument starting and quickly changed the subject. "Sofo, who was the first person you painted? The Queen?"

Sofo laughed. "No, no. I didn't dare risk disgracing myself right off with a painting the king might not have liked. I picked one of Queen Isabella's noble ladies-in-waiting, and promptly got into a whole aspect of painting I wasn't really used to."

"What was that?"

"Jewelry, beads, lace. When the Spanish sat for a portrait, they put on their finest and expected it to stand out in every detail in the painting. That made for really hard work. Each and every jewel on a string of beads had to seem like the real thing, and every strand of beautiful lace as well as its intricate pattern had to look just as it really was. When lace was thrown loosely over bare shoulders so that it had many folds, or as a mantilla over a head, it became a painter's nightmare.

"Painting the noble lady took me what seemed like forever, twice as long as I usually took for a portrait. I took a chance and did what I had with many Italian portraits, even though the Spanish seemed so formal. I had her seated on a bench under a pomegranate tree and eating one of its fruit. When I finally finished, and for all my success, I have to admit I suffered the worst anxieties. What would the king think? But he so loved it that he asked me to do a portrait of his sister Juana, and also of his son Don Carlos, who was sixteen.

"The boy turned out to be the most difficult person I ever painted. He was physically deformed and ugly, which I tried to hide as much as possible. He always wore the most hatefully cruel expression, and was a little crazy, and dreadfully spoiled."

"Ouch," I said. "In other words, he was a real horror."

"He certainly was," Sofo agreed. "He had illusions of grandeur and insisted on being painted with a sword. I was always frightened he'd suddenly decide to use it on me. Eventually, to everyone's relief, Phillip had him locked away when he discovered Don Carlos had been plotting against him. Of course, I then painted King Phillip and, after him, Queen Isabella. His portrait is today considered perhaps the best ever done of him, and hers was and still is my favorite of all my works. She was so beautiful, and everything she was, the inner Isabella, shows in her face.

"That was just the beginning. Word got around, and I found myself with one commission after another. Every nobleman or wealthy financier wanted a portrait of himself or of his wife and his children." Sofo paused to laugh and shake her head. "And do you know?—I still can't quite believe it—King

Phillip told me to charge them a lot, and so I did, and I began to build up a small fortune for myself.

"So time flew. It was Spain's golden age. In spite of all the wars and turmoil, art and literature flourished. It was a time when some of its greatest public buildings and palaces were planned and built. Spain abounded in artists—the greats like El Greco; Murillo and Velázquez would come shortly after I left. And there were the great writers while I was there, too—Cervantes, who wrote *Don Quixote;* Pedro de Barca; and Lope de Vega, who wrote scores of sonnets and eighteen hundred plays. Yes, eighteen hundred, can you imagine? Besides painting. I read myself silly the whole time I was there.

"During my stay, two important things happened. First, I was appointed governess to the royal princess, the Infanta Clara Eugenia. And then to Queen Isabella's second child, Catherine Michelle."

Elvira giggled. "Artist to nanny. Did you have to wear a uniform?"

Sofo smiled indulgently. "Don't be silly." She nudged her silent. "Being royal governess was a highly exalted and honored position that meant I was officially in charge of raising the royal children. And 'in charge' meant how they were educated, where and how they lived, all of that. In short, I was to be their surrogate mother, which made me the social equal of everyone in the royal court, including the king and queen. It brought me all sorts of very special privileges, too: my own dressmaker and hair stylist, my own staff and carriage and bodyguard if I went out, and a very big increase in my pay. It also gave me a kind of absolute authority. To my astonishment, and I never got over it, I suddenly found my word or wish was like law, as much as if I had been the queen or king.

"That was the good thing that happened. The second was a bad thing." The light suddenly disappeared from Sofo's eyes, and her expression became terribly sad. "Tragedy struck," she said. "Queen Isabella died in the birth of her second child. I had become as close to her as I ever was with my own sisters, and I was shattered. To nobody's surprise, so was her husband. He adored her. Whenever she was sick, he was constantly by her side, and when she produced her first child, a girl instead of a boy, he told the whole world how pleased he was.

"For a while the court was in deep mourning. But in a year, Phillip, like so many well married men whose wives have died, began to think of another wife. His son Don Carlos had also died, and he badly needed a male heir. He chose Anna of Austria, who was only fourteen and his niece but politically to his benefit, and they were married by proxy. I was still at court when she arrived, and I saw immediate chemistry between them. Phillip fell madly in love with her, and eventually they were to have four sons and a daughter.

"I wasn't in Spain then, however, for my whole life had suddenly changed. It was just as well because when Elisabeth died, things were never quite the same again. I liked Anna, but we never became great friends. The older children were suddenly grown up, too, and no longer in need of a governess. Besides all that, strangely enough, I had suddenly started being homesick."

"After all those years? Weird."

"Yes, it was, and since I never was one to sit about feeling miserable, I took a giant step to change my life."

"What? What?"

Elvira laughed. "Next time."

Sofo gave me a warm smile and stood up. "She's right. It's getting late."

How I hated these endings and then, worse, the suspense that followed when I didn't know exactly when I would be able to get back to the church. Christmas was coming, and Dad and Arielle and I were getting asked to parties and pre-Christmas celebrations. On top of all that, there were Christmas presents to be bought, and that meant shopping in Henley.

I was lucky, though, and was back in the churchyard the very next day to find the church door open and both my ghostly friends waiting for me in their usual places on the altar steps.

It was early still, the sun not long up. There was only an occasional small white cloud in the winter sky against which the bare branches of trees around the churchyard seemed like giant gnarled fingers stretching upward.

"How on earth did you know I was coming?" I asked.

Elvira laughed mischievously, and Sofo smiled, then became serious and dove right in. "All right. My love life." She thought a moment, then said, "So there I was. It was 1570, I was thirty-six years old, rich as Croesus and famous but unmarried. In my day, like Elvira's, if you weren't married by the time you were seventeen, you were considered over the hill, a hopeless spinster no man in his right mind would want. Things hadn't changed much since Matilda's day. In a world in which everything was men, a woman didn't stand a chance alone and without male protection. So I had started to worry about my future. I had my eye on one rather dashing Italian, Fabrizio de Moncada. He was the son of the Viceroy of Sicily and available. I can't say I was desperately in love with Fabrizio, not the way I had fallen for some of the young artists back in Rome and Florence and couldn't live without them for one second. I'd learned since that the passionate love every young girl dreams of often doesn't last. Much better for the long haul is a responsible, intelligent provider you truly like and trust as a friend, and who you know will be a good father as well as a considerate and caring husband.

"I liked Fabrizio a lot. He was a fine and decent man, marvelously educated, and he clearly thought the world of me. I was wise enough to know how lucky I would be to have him, and when he and I exchanged letters after we met at a Spanish court function, and to one of his questions I wrote back "yes," I found myself engaged. There almost was a snag, however. Without my knowing it, King Phillip, who had long worried for my future, had gone ahead and lined up a nobleman of great wealth whom he and Isabella thought suitable."

"What did you do?"

"Thanked him, of course. Profusely. And said 'no thanks.'"

"And what did he say? Was he very angry?"

"I was afraid he would be. In fact, I was sure I would be politely dismissed. Phillip was always warmly kind to me, but after all, a king is a king, right? To my surprise, he did just the opposite. He was incredibly gracious and not only congratulated me but presented me with an enormous sum of money as my dowry."

"Crumbs," Elvira muttered. "Maybe if my Dad had put up a few shillings for my dowry, I would have found some way to stay alive."

'You wouldn't have needed a dowry," Sofo said. "Whomever you married would have been the richest man in England just to get you."

Elvira bubbled with instant mirth. "Incorrigible and all?"

"That, too."

Sofo put her arm around Elvira's shoulder, and Elvira leaned her head against Sofo. I hurried to get us back on track. Right away, I wanted to know if there'd been a big wedding.

"Big enough. And that's putting it mildly. King Phillip didn't believe in doing things in a small way. I think half of Spain must have been in the cathedral, and the celebrations went on for days. It was fully a month before Fabrizio and I were on our way back to Italy, first to visit my family in Cremona, then to his home in Sicily."

I thought of Matilda's arranged marriage, and how lucky she'd been to have fallen in love with a man who loved her in return. And I thought of all I'd heard about marriages that hadn't turned out that way. I hauled out my courage from somewhere and asked Sofonisba if she ever had any regrets at not being still single. Her answer was as though she'd read my mind.

"None at all," she said. "My years with Fabrizio were truly happy ones."

"Did you ever go back to Spain?" Elvira asked. Since she never had been married, and never could be, she wasn't really interested in the marriage scene, only the romance that preceded it.

"Quite soon, yes. And stayed there for years more. This time to paint King Phillip's new and fourth wife, Anna of Austria, whom at first, as I said, I wasn't close to but whom I grew to like a great deal. She saw me as an older woman—well, I was nearly fifteen years older—whom she looked to for advice. I painted her four children as well. And then, Alicia … then …"

"Then what, what?"

"Next time. Meanwhile, don't do anything I wouldn't do."

"Sofo!" I cried. "That's not fair."

But it was too late. With a light laugh, Sofo

abruptly disappeared. And I thought, yipes! She's just as bad with the teasing as Elvira. No matter how wonderful and important Sofo was and how much I really liked her, I began to feel slightly annoyed, until Elvira said, before she, too, disappeared, that the next session with Sofo would be the last.

"I think she's going to tell you that true love— the passionate kind she warned you not to trust— flew in the window at her," she said. "And when she least expected it." She went unusually thoughtful for a moment and then said, "Love can come at you awfully fast sometimes, and right out of the blue."

"Did that happen to you?" I asked. I sensed somehow that it had.

Elvira didn't answer for a moment, and I was sure I saw tears in her eyes. "Yes," she finally replied softly. "Once."

"But what happened?"

"His family found out I was an uneducated nobody and shipped him off someplace to get over me."

"And did he?"

"I don't know. I never saw him again. And—and then I was betrothed and died."

"Oh, what a downer, Elvira. I'm sorry." I wanted to go and put my arms around her, but I knew I couldn't, and perhaps Elvira might not want me to. So she just sat and stared at nothing. Once I was sure I heard her sniff back tears.

Suddenly the gate in the old brick wall creaked open. I heard Elvira say, "Uh-oh. The vicar after all."

I looked over at the gate and saw him, and

when I looked back, Elvira was gone. As the elderly vicar made his slow way toward the church door, he stopped to wave his cane. "Hello there, back again, are you. Lovely day we're having."

"Yes, sir."

"If you need anything, I'll be in the vestry writing my sermon for tomorrow's service. Tomorrow's Sunday, you know."

"Yes, sir. Thank you."

When the church door had closed behind him, I got up, wondering if love had ever found the dear old man when he was young. Then, seeing Henry, I remembered Elvira asking me if I could get her gravestone righted.

"Henry" I said, "This fallen gravestone …"

"Yes, Miss. Too heavy for me to get back up alone, and the vicar's not too strong these days."

"I'm strong," I said. "Maybe the two of us …"

Henry gave me a cautious look. "Of course, Miss." He fetched a shovel and a pick from his wheelbarrow and dug a narrow trench the width of the stone at one end of the grave where there had clearly once been one.

As he worked, I felt a shiver run through me. Of what? Fear? Excitement? Anxiety? I'd never thought the stone was perhaps lying face down. I'd always thought the inscription had just worn away. Suppose it hadn't, and I'd discover this wasn't Elvira's grave after all. Then an even more disturbing thought struck me. Suppose Henry, digging down, were to strike Elvira's bones.

For what seemed forever plus, I held my breath until a relieved "okay" came from Henry. He put down the spade, and together we wrestled the heavy stone slowly upright and jockeyed it a little until one end dropped down into the narrow slot he'd dug.

"There you go, Miss." Henry stood back and admired our work. "Been dead a while, this one," he said and then tipped his cap and went back to his other chores.

I was already on my knees on the cold, half frozen earth in front of the stone where its weight had long ago killed any grass. Holding my breath, I brushed away dirt stuck to its surface and bit by bit began to see the shallow remains of an inscription, protected from being completely weathered away by the stone's lying flat. But it took more brushing before I found myself staring at the barely visible name Elvira Brown and the dates beneath it, 1573–1588.

It really rocked me. For a moment I thought I was going to pass out. And when I didn't, when I finally sat back down in the dirt where the stone had lain, I was overwhelmed with sadness. Elvira was truly dead. I could only know her as a ghost. I couldn't ever be with her except in the churchyard. We couldn't walk around Henley together, or go to the movies, or buy ice cream, and she couldn't come to my house for a sleepover. What was I going to do when I went back to America? I would probably never see her again.

I couldn't help it. I began to cry. I cared so much about her I thought my heart would break. Poor Elvira. As I grew older, she would always stay the same. She'd always be the wonderful pixyish not quite grown-up yet that she was when she died. She would never be able to fall in love, or marry and have children and grow old with someone, and enjoy everything that could be found in the rainbow of sadness and joy that was a long life.

After a while, I dried tears I knew Elvira would never tolerate, and made my way out of the churchyard. At the sagging old gate in the mossy brick wall I stopped for a last look back at Elvira's gravestone. A strange thought struck me, and in spite of myself, I began to laugh when it suddenly occurred to me that my ghostly friends would no longer have any place to sit except on dirt if they wanted to sit again by the grave itself. And as I got on my bike I thought, well, maybe since they are ghosts, they won't care.

FIVE

"*I* think it was 1578," Sofonisba said, "when King Phillip kindly acceded to my wishes to return to Italy permanently. I'd painted everyone in sight several times over, and Fabrizio wasn't at all happy in the Spanish court. He found gloomy."

It had turned surprisingly warm, almost spring-like. We had favored the churchyard for the church itself, and she was seated on one of the straw beach mats I had found in the church tool shed. Elvira was seated next to her. Overjoyed at her gravestone finally being back up, she bubbled over with laughter, claiming it far superior to all the other gravestones in the churchyard.

"Please, Elvira, I want to hear," I said, and presently she calmed down enough for Sofo to continue her story.

"We went to Fabrizio's home in Palermo, Sicily," Sofo said. "It was palatial. I was waited on hand and foot, the countryside was lovely, the nobility hospitable and friendly, and for the most part well-educated. Fabrizio was quite content at my being an artist and quite unlike the other women in his life: his mother, his sisters, various cousins, and the wives of men friends. All of them had had it drummed into them that a woman's place was to stay silently at home, bear children, and do her husband's bidding."

"Did you paint any of them?"

"A few, yes. But I was reluctant to do so, actually, because it exposed me totally as an artist, and unlike them, which I felt would be in a way flying in their faces. I always thought their accepting that Fabrizio had married a woman who was 'different' was enough. Why push my luck?"

Sofo paused, seeing an odd expression on my face. "Something about it bothers you. What is it?"

I hesitated. I didn't want to seem rude. "Well ..."

"Come on," Sofo urged. "Out with it. We're friends."

"Well," I blurted out, "everything you say makes it sound like you felt like a fish out of water. I mean, how could you have been happy living like that?"

Sofonisba laughed. "Clever you. You saw right through me, didn't you? You're right. I wasn't happy, although to be honest, I wasn't really unhappy either. I think my chief emotion was boredom. Excitement in my life, when my life had truly been *my* life, had suddenly ground to a halt. In Palermo all I felt was dullness. I never wanted to get up, no matter how beautiful the day or whatever Fabrizio had planned. I just wanted to pull the covers over my head and sink into memories of Florence and home in Cremona and Rome, when I had the endless thrill of working with crusty old Michelangelo."

"Did you have any children?"

"No, although we tried. I was given every sort of herb and potion by an old witch Fabrizio dug up somewhere and whom all the common folk of Palermo swore by, but nothing happened."

"It's because you didn't want any," Elvira suddenly interjected.

Sofonisba turned on her first with a look of sharp surprise then with a warm smile. "You, young lady, are as clever as Alicia. The pair of you have looked right into me. And you are right. Not that I realized it, of course. I thought I wanted children, but my unconscious mind said 'no.'"

"But why?" I protested. "I mean wouldn't having children have created excitement for you?"

"I suppose, but the simple truth of it all was that I didn't *love* Fabrizio. Like him, respect him, admire him, yes. Appreciate his kindness to me, yes. But *love*? No. And a woman, if she feels a real sense of independence about herself and is as unconventional as I was, and not content to be just a *wife*, has to feel some sort of passion for her husband if she is going to accept him as the father of her children. My mind had never been trained to bow down to all the rigid social rules that applied to other women of my time.

I had no passion for the man I married. Without realizing it at the time, mostly because I was so concerned about my age and never having been married, I had done what almost every woman did back then, which was totally against my character—tie myself up for life to someone because of the need for protection and security. Or because it was insisted on by the social codes."

"You were lucky to have a father who believed in your talent and who helped you become so independent," I said, at the same time thinking that in spite of all the laughing and deviltry, how very shrewd Elvira was. Her lack of education hadn't prevented her from understanding life and people. Or perhaps it was the harsh and often brutal life she had led in her short few years that had given her so much insight into others. I was snapped back from my thoughts when I heard her say to Sofo, "I remember you once told me that true love flew right in the window at you when you least expected it."

"You mean that I had a big love in my life?"

"You told me you had," Elvira said accusingly.

"Well, you're right. I did."

"When? How? Who was he?" Elvira and I both spoke at once.

Laughing, Sofo held up an arresting hand. "Wait. Both of you. I was just coming to that."

So I sat back while Sofo collected her thoughts. "Okay. I had been married to Fabrizio for just a little over eight years," she finally said, "when fate stepped in to change my whole life again. It was in the summer of 1579, and on one of those glorious Mediterranean summer days, which for me was at first like every other day, except we had all been worried about reports of a plague sweeping through towns not far from Palermo, even though in our palace there was little chance of a plague striking, since Fabrizio was fanatically fussy about sanitation and cleanliness. Workmen in filthy clothes weren't allowed through the front gates. They had to come scrubbed clean and in their Sunday best. As for rats or mice, they simply weren't allowed. If one was found, every servant was punished from the steward to the lowliest kitchen maid.

"Well, I was out in the garden, seated beneath a lovely old pomegranate tree and reading, when I suddenly became aware of my personal maid standing before me. She was sheet-white and twisting one hand in the other. In a choked voice, she was trying to say something which I soon realized was my husband's name. My book, the glorious day, even where I was, were instantly forgotten. I leapt to my feet, and I think I knew Fabrizio was dead even before my maid fainted. Her dread news was confirmed by the palace steward, who rushed out a few moments after her.

"There'd been a boating accident. He'd gone sailing with two friends in a little dory, and it had been run down by the thoughtless captain of a huge bireme."

"Oh, but that's awful, Sofo. What's a bireme?"

"A bireme was a galley, except it had two decks of oarsmen."

"They didn't exist anymore in my day," Elvira said.

"No. The discovery of America and oceangoing naval vessels put an end to them. Anyway, so there I was, a widow," Sofo said, "and at age forty-six. I stayed on in Palermo for what I thought was a respectful and decent interlude. I really had no place else to go. I liked Sicily. I loved my home, and to be honest, I felt a sort of freedom in it once Fabrizio was no longer there. I was urged by King Phillip to return to Spain, but I didn't go. I felt that chapter of my life was like a book that you no longer have need to open once you've finished it.

"Soon, I guess in about a year, I yearned to see Cremona again, and decided on a visit. The trip by land would take weeks over terrible and sometimes dangerous roads. I decided to go by sea and set sail from Palermo on a chilly autumn morning."

"Was it a galley again?"

"No. Not this time. It was an oceangoing vessel, one of a large fleet owned by a prominent Genovese nobleman, Orazio Lomellino, that sailed out of Genoa, the great Mediterranean seaport on Italy's northwest coast. We set sail, and I had hardly settled in my cabin when there was a knock at the door and my maid admitted Orazio himself. He had come to make certain that my 'famous personage had found everything to her satisfaction.'"

At the memory, Sofonisba broke into delighted laughter. "And well," she said. "That was it. Standing in the doorway smiling down at me was the most beautiful man I had ever met or even thought existed. I was instantly so in love, even though I was a good ten years older than he, as to be helpless if he so much as looked at me. Dining at his captain's table, I felt as though I were sixteen all over again. I became so shy I could hardly speak. Because of a storm, we stopped off at Sardinia for five days, where he arranged for me to stay at the home of the viceroy. And then, before I knew it, three weeks had gone by as though in a dream, and we were entering the busy port of Genoa.

"I was standing near the helm with Orazio in a state of total distress at the thought of parting from him, perhaps forever, when something in me suddenly snapped. I suppose it was the real inner me who had tigered her way up to the top of the entirely male art world. I turned to face him, seized his two shoulders, and said, "Orazio, for three weeks I haven't been able to sleep and hardly able to eat, I am so in love. Would you do me the enormous honor of becoming my husband?"

"Wow! Far out. What did he say?"

"You know, Alicia, to this day I have no idea. All I can remember is his lovely smile, the kisses he bestowed on my hands, and our marriage in the cathedral at Genoa."

Elvira clapped her hands with delight. "And they lived happily ever after."

"You are *so* right. We did, and he was the most wonderful loving husband any woman could ever hope for. He encouraged me endlessly in my work. He even went out and found people who wanted portraits painted. His pride in me knew no limits. Of course, we lived like royalty. I was very rich, and he was also. We had the loveliest *palazzo* imaginable in Genoa where his family, whom I adored, joined us, and where I had a huge studio all of my own, and all the time in the world to paint. We also spent a good deal of time in Palermo, especially in the winter, when even Genoa would get quite cold. We entertained lavishly, but not just titled nobility. Our guests were mostly poets, writers, other painters, and sculptors and architects. We virtually had an open house, and I helped many a young artist get started and established the same way Vasari and Michelangelo had helped me."

"Did you ever get back to Cremona?"

"Yes, of course. And saw my sister Minerva, who was deeply respected for the scholarly works she had created, and I visited the convent where my dear sister Elena had taken her vows. And of course I also visited the graves of my parents. And so, children, that's how this lucky artist spent the rest of her days, forty years, in fact, with a loving husband who looked after me as tenderly when I was a very old woman in her nineties as when we were first married."

"Ninety? I can't believe it. You lived that long?"

"I did. Until I was ninety-six, actually, when my heart finally gave out in Palermo, where we had gone because of the warmth. It was there that I was visited and painted by the great Flemish artist, Van Dyck, with whom I discussed art endlessly and to whom I gave many a long hour of instruction. In his portrait of me, which is quite famous, you can definitely see my technique. Yes, dear children, I continued working right to the end, even though I was half blind. After all, a true artist never retires. If you'd like to see some of my work, you'll have to visit the Prado in Madrid, or the Uffizi in Florence, or the Venetian Gallery in Venice, and one of my favorite works is in England in the gallery of the Earl of Spencer, Winston Churchill. There are other important works in the Hermitage in St. Petersburg in Russia and in the national museum in Berlin. My first important portrait, me and my teacher in Cremona, Bernardino Campi, is in the gallery in Siena in Italy."

There was a long moment's silence. Then Sofo stood up. "Alicia, I hate drawn-out farewells. I just want to say how I've loved visiting you. Perhaps we will have the chance to meet again. I really hope so. Elvira, take good care of her. She's important."

She blew me a kiss.

"Wait! Sofo!"

But it was too late. Sofonisba Anguissola had disappeared, and I spent the week miserable at her absence, the same way I had when Matilda went back to the spirit world.

End of Part Two

Lucie Dillon, La Marquise de la Tour de Pin

ONE

Christmas stopped everything, and then quite suddenly, with no warning, we all had to fly back to America for Dad's work. Worse, we stayed there until almost spring, with Dad endlessly meeting with his new editor and also contracting to edit the book of another writer. It was spring before we returned to England, and the flood of relief I felt when Dad said we'd be going back to the same wonderful yellow brick house in the Thames Valley sent me into a state of euphoria nobody could understand. I could hardly tell them the reason for it.

We'd hardly been back a day when I found a chance to race to the old Norman church and its lovely churchyard with its friendly old gravestones and crosses weathered gray with age. It was a perfect day for the meeting. The vicar never came on Saturday mornings, Elvira had told me, because he always spent them getting his sermon ready for Sunday, and then he went up to Henley for lunch. Full spring was rushing over England in a wave of warmth and fresh color, and Henry was already busy raking up winter debris and tending to jonquils and crocuses. He seemed an old friend, and I felt a rush of warm feeling for him. I said, "Hello," he tipped his hat, and I waited until he'd gone to a far corner of the churchyard and then rushed straight to Elvira's grave. I sketched until Henry left and then called out, "Elvira, it's me. It's me." And waited.

Suddenly she was there, and so casually that it was hard to believe months had gone by since we last met. "Ah, there you are," she said. "You took long enough."

I babbled an explanation and she pretended haughtiness and said. "Oh, sure, sure. I bet actually the only reason you came at all is to know Lucie Dillon and how she escaped the guillotine."

I'd started to bristle. Hadn't she missed me? But that stopped me. "Lucie who? Who is she?"

"La Marquise de la Tour de Pin. You don't know about her?"

"Who, what?"

Elvira laughed gaily. "She was the daughter of an Irishman commanding one of the French King Louis VI's most important armies, and a lady-in-waiting to Marie Antoinette. Come the revolution in France in 1785 with all that *Terror*, off-with-their-heads stuff, she and her husband barely escaped the guillotine. Matilda and Sofo and I decided she would be a good person for you to meet."

That stopped me again, and before I could collect myself, Elvira said, "Tell you what. Go to the library and read up on her. That will save me a lot of introduction."

With that, she promptly disappeared, and there was nothing for it but that I do as she said.

Lucy herself, I read, was half Irish, and although born in England, she was raised in France. Her father was a titled lord and the famed colonel of a private regiment hired out to the French king, Louis XV. Through a French branch of the family, her uncle was an archbishop whose *see* was the whole southern part of France, known as the Vendée. Her mother's family were one of the oldest and most revered noble families in France and closely related to royalty for centuries past. Portraits of her made her look blond and interesting, but much more important to me than how she looked was, what would she be like? During her life, I read, she was considered by her peers as brilliantly intelligent a woman who could hold her own with the best minds of the day in science and philosophy, and a woman of unparalleled personal courage as well. At the same time, she was universally liked and was shrewdly political in coping with the endless intrigues of her time. When she fled the revolution, she and her husband farmed in America for several years, and she actually milked the cows and did all the dairy work herself, as well as helping in the fields, plowing, and harvesting and, according to her own diaries, loved every minute of it.

I also read about the dreaded guillotine. It was

the ghastly machine invented to decapitate, and during the revolution was used to execute over forty-five thousand completely innocent people. Brought from prison in rough carts and pelted with filth by howling mobs, they were dragged up onto a scaffold and forced face-down on a plank between high upright tracks, between which a huge razor-sharp knife like a cleaver would rattle down onto their necks.

When it came to actually meeting her, as I waited the next afternoon by Elvira's gravestone for her to appear with Elvira, I felt more than my usual nervousness on meeting anyone new, ghost or not. Would she be as down-to-earth as Matilda and Sofonisba? Or would she be an awful snob? And what would she think of me? I wasn't ever going to win any beauty contests.

"Alicia? Wake up."

I snapped out of wallowing in a reverie of semi self-pity to see Elvira right in front of me, and with her a tall, slender, college-age woman with a mass of luxurious blond hair that tumbled down over her shoulders and around a pleasant open face. I realized I'd been looking right at them both without seeing them.

"Goodness, where were you?" Elvira demanded.

The woman with her smiled warmly. She wasn't beautiful but she had perfect teeth and hazel eyes that I felt she could see right through me the way I could actually see right through her to the churchyard behind her. She said, "Daydreaming, which is what I always do. Hello, Alicia. I'm Lucie."

"Actually Henrietta-Lucie Dillon, Madame Gouvernet, La Marquise de la Tour de Pin," Elvira offered.

Lucie laughed. "Enough of that. Just plain Lucie will do, thank you." Her voice was soft and lightly touched with a French accent. "And I'm so glad to meet an American again. So please feel at home with me." With that she plunked herself down on the grass next to Elvira and sat cross-legged, looking up at me. So I sat down too. Or, to be more accurate, collapsed.

I knew at one that I was going to like her. She looked exactly the way I had thought she might look—regal. There was something else, too. She radiated a kind of down-to-earth self-confidence that had nothing to do with being high-born or famous. She reminded me of the head nurse in the hospital emergency room when I broke my arm skateboarding and who had quickly taken charge of everything and everyone, Mom and Dad, too, and they both did whatever she said until the doctor came.

"And, Alicia," she added, "since I died at seventy-five, I decided to come at the age when most of my story took place, the way Elvira tells me Sofo did. Is that all right with you?"

I didn't hesitate to say yes, she made me feel that comfortable, and I dove right in and asked how she had ended up farming when she'd been a lady-in-waiting to Marie Antoinette.

'We have to go back a bit," Lucie replied. "What do you know about the French Revolution?"

"Not much," I offered. "Except they kicked out

the king and executed a lot of people with the guillotine, and burned down the Bastille. That was a huge fortress prison in Paris, right?"

"Right, and a hated symbol of royal power, even though the very few prisoners in it were mostly aristocrats who'd been put there for minor offenses or bad behavior. Some of them were even waited on by servants they brought with them. That was on July 14, 1789, thirteen years *after* your declaration of independence. In France it's often known as *Bastille Day,* and it celebrates French independence, although the actual getting rid of the monarchy, by executing Louis XVI, came quite a bit later."

"But how did it all start? I mean, the revolution. What caused it?" I asked, remembering the total power of kings and royalty that I'd learned about from Matilda and Sofonisba. The way the feudal system worked, I couldn't imagine the common people simply rising up like that. "It didn't just happen overnight, did it?"

"Not at all," Lucie replied. "And there were all sorts of reasons. First, all of Europe was still under the reign of monarchs whose word, even thoughts, were considered divine and never questioned. All during the seventeen and eighteenth centuries, writers and philosophers had begun to challenge this, and people began to want to determine their own destinies. The result of your remarkable revolution in 1776 was talked about everywhere.

"In the terrible winter of 1788 and 1789 there was poverty throughout all of Europe, and with the failure of the two previous years' harvests, food was dangerously short. People in some countries were faced with famine, especially in France, where King Louis XVI's father had nearly emptied the national treasury on unnecessary wars and lavish living, and Louis had continued the same way. Rumblings of discontent grew louder, especially in Paris, but the king was oblivious to them.

"But how he could he be? He was right there, wasn't he? Didn't he have eyes?"

"He had eyes, all right, but he wasn't there, and that was the problem. He and his *court,* which was the government, was at a place called Versailles. Ten miles of open country, forests and fields, separated it from the city of Paris, which was very small compared to today, and except for the homes of the rich nobility was mostly a damp, overcrowded, and disease-ridden little city of about half a million people, most of whom could neither read nor write. There were none of the many magnificent avenues and beautiful buildings one so associates with the Paris of today. The Champs-Élysées was a country dirt track; the site of the now famed Arc de Triomphe was haunted by robbers and highwaymen. Many streets were so narrow that the houses nearly shut out the sun and, if not cobbled, were mostly open sewers.

"Versailles, on the other hand, was quite a different story. The royal palace, known as *Le Château,* occupied sixteen and a half acres and was the wonder of all Europe."

"Wow! That's huge."

"It certainly was. Building it, along with its thousand acres of gardens, paved courtyards, fountains, and, yes, even lakes, took seven thousand men and a thousand horses over forty years. The court there numbered several thousand nobility and clergy and had a lifestyle that was as far removed as could be imagined from the lives of everyone else in France. It was more opulent, frivolous, and decadent than anything seen anywhere before or since. They were oblivious to everything except themselves. Every night there were huge banquets and balls lit by thousands of candles, where the women were so laden with jewelry they could hardly stand. Nobody rose until mid-morning or later, and then did nothing the rest of the day and late into the next night but indulge in endless intrigue and gossip. Every day, while the rest of the country starved, the court consumed enough of the finest foods and drank enough expensive wine to keep an army on the march for weeks, and was waited on hand and foot by over three thousand servants."

"Three thousand?" I tried to imagine that and couldn't.

"There were many more servants than nobility."

"The women spent hours every day on their hair," Elvira said. "They covered it with powder and pomade and jewels and piled it way up high on their heads a foot tall."

"Like some sort of towering headdress," Lucie added. "A woman scarcely dared move for fear it would all come down. Most women had their own personal hairdresser. A whole morning was spent, right up until dinner at one or two in the afternoon, getting ready. And what clothes! You can't imagine. Silks and satins and brocades that kept hundreds of seamstresses forever busy because there were nearly always two changes in dress every day, one for morning, one for afternoon, and sometimes a third for evening wear. Most of us rarely ever wore the same thing more than twice. We were corseted in at the waist until we could hardly breathe, and with women seen very much as sex objects, the dresses were cut as low as decency permitted. As for the skirts, they were voluminous. They were held out far from your legs by a cage of hoops, called a *panier*, which were so large that sometimes it was difficult to get through even wide doorways. I remember the Queen herself got stuck in one, and there was the most dreadful rush to extricate her."

I couldn't help exclaiming how awful it all sounded. "Didn't anyone work?"

"Work? Goodness, no. Nobody in the nobility or clergy *ever* worked."

"But where did their money come from?"

"The poor," Elvira said. "Who else?"

"Exactly. Nobility got their money from their properties, agriculture or vineyards, mostly, where all the work was done by others and where all who were the tenants had to pay exorbitant rents as well as render part of their produce."

Elvira broke in again to ask what the queen was like.

"Marie Antoinette? She was Austrian, the sister

of the Austrian emperor. When she came to France, she was young and beautiful and loved by everyone. She died, hated by all and with her looks badly injured by arrogance and hopeless vanity. I really don't think she ever thought of anyone but herself. She had no concept of any life except the glitter of the court where, right or wrong, she was always 'right' and where everyone fell over themselves seeking her favors. She didn't even dress or bathe herself. Her ladies-in-waiting did that for her. We also remade her bed with fresh linen every day. Four footmen, wearing white gloves so their naked hands wouldn't contaminate anything they touched, came first to turn the heavy mattress."

"They did the same for the king," Elvira said. "Can you imagine a man who couldn't dress himself?"

"And be given a bath like a child?" Lucie said. "But for all that, the king himself was not a bad man, even though stupid and far removed from reality. When he finally realized the country was broke and at the mercy of its enemies, he called the Estates General into an emergency session."

"What was that?"

"The Estates General was an assembly composed of three different groups, or estates, and was originally formed a century before to advise the king on taxes. Louis hoped they would find a way to pay off the nation's debts. The *First* and *Second Estates* were the *Church* and the *nobility,* who, with the king, owned all the property in France. Between them, they had hundreds of votes."

"What about the Third?"

"The *Third Estate* was everybody else: ninety per-cent of France, the peasantry and workers and all the middle class. It had just one vote."

"But that means they couldn't have their say in anything," I cried.

"Exactly, "Lucie replied. "And that was the whole idea. The First and Second Estates, who were rolling in money, could vote to pay no taxes themselves, and dump the whole tax burden on the Third, who were already taxed half to death."

I started an indignant protest, but Lucie held up a hand. "Hold on. By cleverly using the terrible finan-cial crisis and the sheer weight of their numbers, the Third Estate turned the tables. They declared them-selves the *National Assembly*, and the nobility could join them or not, as they wished. They got the sup-port from several cities and some of the clergy, along with a few of the nobility—men like Lafayette, who saw opportunity in it for themselves."

"Was that the same Lafayette who helped us in our revolution?"

"Yes. But he was not liked in France the way he was in your country. He was considered out for him-self only and wasn't trusted."

That surprised me, but I didn't question it. I was too curious to know what happened next to get side tracked. "So what happened then?" I asked.

"As usual, essentially nothing. The nobility con-tinued to dance the nights away, there was end-less noise and uproar in the great assembly hall at

Versailles as this new National Assembly argued use-lessly and decided nothing, and the people got hungrier and hungrier.

"There were many among the clergy and nobility, however, who saw the handwriting on the wall and began to leave the country. They were called the *émigrés*, and their flight to England and the Netherlands enraged the National Assembly, who saw them spiriting money from the country when it was most needed.

"Matters finally came to a head when the king fired his Swiss minister of finance for daring to propose taxing the never-taxed clergy and the nobility. It was good news for the nobility, of course. They celebrated—but when I went to bed that night, I had an awful sense of an impending storm. I was young and vain and complacent, yes, and mostly concerned with my toilette—how my hair was dressed, what my clothes looked like. But I had always read a lot, and not just the usual romantic poetry considered suitable for ladies, but science and especially history. I had studied your American Revolution. I felt there had to be a reaction, perhaps even a violent one. And I was right. Life at court went on as usual, but it didn't elsewhere. Fears grew that the king would try to dissolve the National Assembly and take away the people's newfound power, and on July 14, 1789, an enraged Parisian mob, seeking the weapons stored there, burned down the Bastille."

"Understandable," I ventured. "Where were you when it happened? At Versailles?"

"No. I was married by then, and while my husband

was away on military duty with his regiment, I was living with my aunt in a small house at a far end of the Versailles gardens, half an hour from *Le Château*. I was on my way from there to visit friends on an estate some distance away when a servant on a fast horse caught up to me with the news. I went straight to the palace, where I was sure I'd find panic. But, can you believe it? Nobody seemed even remotely concerned. There were rumors, of course—the Marquis de Lafayette had ordered the Bastille burned down to appease the mob, there had been a massacre, and the Hôtel de Ville—that was the town hall in Paris—had also been attacked and the mayor murdered. People just shrugged them off, however. Lafayette would restore order, they said, with a new military force called the National Guard. And so the court danced the night away once again, and indeed, the next day everything seemed to have calmed down."

"Did you think things had?"

"No, I didn't. I suspected those who'd attacked the Bastille weren't just rabble. And I was right—there was far worse to come. On October 4th, the King's brother, the Duke of Orléans, who believed the throne rightfully his, sent agents all over Paris stirring things up among the starving poor."

"Lining things up for a coup d'état?" I asked, remembering the phrase from French class at school.

Lucie smiled in delight. "Good for you. There was one in the making, all right."

I was hardly surprised. I'd been well primed by Matilda that loyalty, if you could ever call it that, was virtually nonexistent among royals if not directly tied to money or property. I said, "Was it discovered?"

"Yes and no. Everyone knew, but it was hard to prove. And his plotting did a lot of damage. The National Guard began to break up into different factions, some loyal to the king, others to the duke. The queen didn't help things, either."

I'd almost forgotten Marie-Antoinette. "What did she do," I asked, "other than parade around in jewelry?"

"Just that," Lucie replied. "Except this time it was jewelry and more jewelry in an incident that's famous in French history. On the Feast of Saint Louis every year, she always received traditional delegations from the city of Paris who came to pay homage—the mayor, and all the heads of the various guilds, including the very powerful guild of fishwives. As though deliberately setting out to insult them, she was virtually dressed in diamonds. I mean, her whole dress, from her bosom to her feet, was covered with hundreds and hundreds of them: big ones, small ones, every kind. There were so many you could scarcely see the material they were sewed onto. She glittered in the light. And remember, these were people without enough to eat. Even worse was her manner. She spoke to everyone, if she spoke at all, as though they were dirt, which is what she thought of them. I saw groups, not just workers but bankers, lawyers, businessmen, even some officers in the new National Guard, all going away in angry silence or muttering to themselves."

"Was that it? I mean, is that what finally pushed things off the cliff?"

"Perhaps, yes," Lucie replied. "And especially where the Fishwives were concerned, as you shall see. We didn't have to wait long to find out, either. News came to *Le Château* that there had been another riot in Paris, and some poor baker, they said, had been hung because he couldn't provide the mob with bread."

Lucie paused, remembering. "Then word came," she said, "that a huge mob of women towing cannons and backed by the Paris branch of the National Guard were marching on Versailles."

"Wow. What happened then?"

"A nightmare. They arrived early in the evening at the Place d'Armes. That was a vast cobbled courtyard as big as several of your football fields that was the entrance to *Le Château* itself. And they were a terrifying sight, those women. They were armed to the teeth with axes and swords and old muskets, and screaming and yelling the most terrible things about the queen. Most of them were in rags and filthy dirty, their hair in greasy tangles, and nearly all were terribly drunk. Of course, nobody in the court had ever seen any people like that. My husband had arrived to bolster the Swiss Guard with a small Versailles branch of the National Guard, which was loyal to him. But several hundred women somehow got into *Le Château* itself."

"Right inside?"

"Right inside, and right up the sweeping marble

main stairway into the great mirrored halls above, lit by a score of huge crystal chandeliers, each with hundreds of candles. The king and queen were hidden away at a far end of *Le Château* in the royal apartments, me along with them. We could hear shouts and pistol shots and the sounds of shattering glass and ransacking, and the screams of several guards who were literally hacked to death with knives and axes. It went on and on and was absolutely terrifying as they tried to batter down doors and drag out anyone hiding. Eventually, it was only when Lafayette came to the rescue, with a large section of the National Guard that was still loyal, that this horrible inhuman mob dispersed, and the exhausted court went to bed.

"But wait—that wasn't the end of it. At dawn a small band found a secret door back into *Le Château.* It had been unlocked, and we always suspected by agents of the Duke of Orléans. Before they could be stopped, this band of horrors got back up into the main galleries and headed for the royal apartments. Fortunately, my husband frantically moved me, still half asleep, to a safer apartment than the one I was in. The king had been urged to leave and had refused, and for both him and Marie Antoinette, it was a very close call.

"When the mob reached the queen's suite, the one guard there held on long enough—before they murdered him—to allow the queen to escape through a secret passageway into the king's apartment some distance away. It took what seemed an eternity for the

National Guard to get this mob out of *Le Château*. There were endless screams and shots and the crashing sound of more breaking glass as they destroyed more priceless mirrors and chandeliers. And in the morning, there was blood splattered everywhere."

"What happened then? I mean, that wasn't the end of it, was it? What about the guillotine and all that?"

"No, no. it wasn't the end at all. It was only a very slight beginning. Amazingly, for most people, even the very poor, it was still 'Long live the King.'"

"I can't believe it."

"Well, it was, but the king just the same was forced to abandon *Le Château* at Versailles as well as all government offices there and move the entire court to Paris, into the great palace of the Tuileries. It was torn down in 1871, but back then it stretched for nearly a thousand feet from the River Seine west to the Rue de Rivoli and sealed off the whole open courtyard, now surrounded on three sides by the great museum of the Louvre."

"But that was huge. It must have been nearly as big as the palace at Versailles."

"Nearly, although without the gardens and lakes. But again, even though living in rags and crowded, starving, and half frozen into one-room hovels, the poor of Paris seemed to accept that as the way things were and always had been."

"Is that where you lived, then? The Tuileries?"

"No. I went with the court, of course, but I lived away from the Tuileries in a beautiful town house of

my aunt in the Rue du Bac across the Seine. That's
the Left Bank, an area now famous for its antique
and art shops and nearby sidewalk cafés along the
Boulevard Saint-Germain. I had a large apartment
of my own and spent a winter that seemed no different from any other. There were dinners and balls and
rides to the theater in my carriage with two footmen,
but I really enjoyed none of it because, regrettably,
both my husband and I were living entirely on the
charity of others."

"Oh? Why?"

"Well, on August 4th, the National Assembly
abolished collecting any revenue from personal property, and there went almost all of my husband's and
my father-in-law's income from their extensive vineyards in southwest France, near the big Atlantic coast
city of Bordeaux. I found myself penniless, too. My
valuable estates in Brittany and Normandy, which
had been my grandfather's and then my mother's and
were my inheritance, were seized even before I was
born by my grandmother when my mother was too
young to protest. She could have saved herself the
trouble because my Uncle, the Archbishop of Nar-
bonne, was a hopeless gambler and guaranteed the
estates against his gambling debts. When he fled
the country as an *émigré*, they were seized by his
creditors."

I tried to add it up. People in a family robbing
each other and especially a child? For a moment, I
just stared. And then blurted out, "Your grandmother
and your uncle?"

Lucie sort of shrugged. "My grandmother was a wicked cruel woman obsessed with greed, my uncle a kindly man with a terrible weakness. There were many like him. The clergy and the Church were a good way to amass wealth."

"What did you do?"

"For money? I sold jewelry and family heirlooms and borrowed from kindly relatives. Among the nobility, it was unthinkable to reduce your lifestyle. But there was far worse to come than being reduced from riches to charity.

"In view of the warning we'd had from the mob attacking Versailles, life as usual can only be seen now as utterly ridiculous. The nobility still just didn't get it. What happened when finally they did is something I will save for our next meeting, when you'll get your fill of the guillotine and the *Terror* that killed off over forty-eight thousand people and turned the whole world upside down."

"But Lucie," Elvira said. "What about yourself? I mean, before all that. You haven't told Alicia anything about your life before you became a lady-in-waiting: your childhood, your marriage. I think you should do that first."

"Oh, okay. I'll briefly go back to the beginning before I tell you about escaping the Terror. Is that all right, Alicia?"

"Yes, please," I said. I had fallen completely under her spell and couldn't hear enough from her.

"It's a promise," Lucie smiled, and then simply vanished.

I was quite startled, which made Elvira laugh. "Alicia, she liked you. I've never heard her talk so much. I think I'm going to learn as much about the revolution as you are."

She blew me a ghostly kiss and, like Lucie, vanished in an instant, leaving me alone in the empty churchyard, which now, with the sun low over the horizon, was beginning to fall into deep shadows.

I made my way back to our big yellow rented house, my head filled with pictures of Versailles Palace, angry fisherwomen and terrified nobility, wondering what would come next. Most of all I wondered how Lucie Dillon, a young Irish woman, only partly French, had come to be a lady-in-waiting to one of history's most infamous queens, who was immortalized when, after being told that the starving poor of France had no bread, she supposedly said, "Let them eat cake."

TWO

When I met Lucie with Elvira the next day, it was raining, and we took refuge in the church. When I worried about the vicar, Elvira told me not to. "He usually enters by the vestry, but this time, if it's the front door, we'll hear him before he puts a hand on the door knob." She laughed. "You can tell him you were praying for a deceased friend."

Lucie told her "Shame," and gave me a radiant smile, and I plunked down in a front pew as I'd always done. "I hope you're prepared to be bored," she continued, "because you wanted to hear the first part of my life, and I've got to confess, it was pretty dreary."

That sort of flummoxed me, so I guess my response wasn't much more than a stupid smile.

"I won't bother you with being born," she said. "That's everyone's unhappy fate or good luck, depending on how you look at it. Where I was concerned, my life, to be honest, was a bit of both. My father, you already know about, Elvira told me. He was famous and very dashing, but as a second cousin had been practically brought up with my mother and was more like a brother to her than a husband. She was a very beautiful woman whom everyone adored. She came from the highest rank of French nobility with blood ties to many of the great titles all over Europe, including royalty. My grandfather's family also dated back for untold centuries, so you might say I was pretty highborn."

With Lucie's father English and her mother French, I had a question, and asked if there were many English-French marriages. "You said the two countries were at war."

"As nations, yes—except nobility married nobility, regardless of nationality, and royalty married royalty in order to consolidate power or for economic reasons, just like in Matilda's time. Love, for the most part, still had nothing to do with it."

I wasn't surprised. It was the same old story of treating women as second-class citizens, leaving guile and wit as their only defense.

"My grandmother was a terrible woman," Lucie went on. "She wielded power and social position, and she ruled with a viciously hurtful tongue. When the queen persuaded my mother to finally protest her theft of my property, she openly turned on my mother with the most appalling and undisguised hatred, and I grew up in an atmosphere that was pure poison.

After my mother died, any protest from me brought threats of my being sent to a convent."

"But where was your father then?"

"He'd gone to the West Indies as governor of St. Kitts. He remarried a Creole, a woman born in the islands who was the mother of my half-sister, Fanny. In his absence, my old fuddy-duddy great-uncle, the Archbishop, as the only man in the household, and at the first sign of one of grandmother's rages, he'd be off to play cards. We lived with him at the great stately home at *Hautefontaine,* and when we wintered in Paris we lived first at my mother's house, which, when my mother died, she sold. We then and we moved to his huge *hôtel,* or town house.

"All this time, my only refuge from my grand-mother was in my studies, which were the same formal training all young ladies of my class received— language, music, handwriting, religious tracts, some Latin, and some elementary math. And of course all the embroidery and sewing. I liked to sew, how-ever, and was an ace at it. It stood me in good stead later when fleeing the Terror. The thing that really saved me, however, was my boundless curiosity. I read everything I could get my hands on, most of it for-bidden to young women. Besides all the famous writ-ers of the Enlightenment, I read numerous scientific tracts, and I taught myself advanced mathematics and calculus."

It all sounded terribly lonely to me, and I ven-tured to say so.

"That's sweet of you, Alicia. Yes, it was. It's hard

living with someone who hates you. Until I married, there were only two people in my life from whom I received affection and support. One was the queen, believe it or not. Arrogant and vain and hopelessly self-centered as she was, still she had been deeply fond of my mother, and she was probably the reason my grandmother didn't dare to send me off to a convent. The other was Marguerite."

The completely new name surprised me. "Who was she?" I asked.

"Marguerite was a young peasant girl brought in to be my personal servant when I was in my early teens. She could neither read nor write but was a woman of true wisdom and incredible courage. Except for the time when I was in America, she was always my closest confidante and intimate through many a sad or dangerous moment. When she died I felt as though my soul had been wrenched from my body."

Lucie was silent a moment, remembering. Then she said, "When I was around sixteen, my grandmother began looking for a husband for me. I was due to take my mother's place as a lady-in-waiting to the queen, but I had to be married first."

Elvira giggled. "So what did she come up with?"

"With a number of attractive and highly eligible young men whom I turned down flat."

"But why?"

"All sorts of reasons, but I think the real one was to defy Grandmother."

That made sense to me, and I was now consumed with curiosity. She'd married the Marquis de la Tour de Pin? How did they meet? What sort of person was he? Given the reasons for marriage back then, I was almost scared to know the truth.

Elvira broke in. "I couldn't have answered any of those questions. My father got hold of me by the neck out in the barn, where I was cleaning out the ox stalls, and said, "Come out of there, you, and get the muck cleaned off yourself. I've found a young fool willing to pay to marry you next week, and he's up to the house with his family to arrange things. I'll be seeing the back o' the likes o' you, thank God, with all you cost me." And for good luck, he gave me a great cuff to the head that made my ears ring."

"Oh, dear," Lucie said. "I'm sorry." She put an arm around Elvira.

"It's all right," Elvira said brightly. "I stuck it to Dad and his plan to be rid of me by up and croaking, and it cost him ten shillings to get me put under."

Lucie, amused at such callous candor, turned to me. "My marriage, I think, began sometime before I ever met Frederick. I'd seen the vast Tour de Pin estates near Bordeaux, with their miles and miles of beautiful vineyards and orchards. I couldn't help but fantasize what it would be like to be mistress of it all.

"When Frederick's name came up, he was still 'Monsieur de Gouvernet'; he wouldn't be the Marquis until his father died. He and his family found both me and what I could bring to them quite suitable. His aunt was Madame d'Henin, the Princesse de Monconseil. She teamed up with the queen herself to push my grandmother into agreeing to a match. Nobody had asked me what I thought, and I astonished everyone, especially my old tormentor, by saying right out that I'd like nothing better."

"But you hadn't even met the man," I protested.

"On top of that," Elvira said," You always told me that he had a bad reputation as a gambler and a general no-good."

"Yes. I heard of all that, but it didn't make any difference. And don't ask why. For some reason I was suffused with romantic feelings. The name Tour de Pin appealed to me as much as the beautiful estates themselves, and I possibly said 'yes' to again defy my grandmother, who didn't find him suitable at all. Just the same, I held my breath until he came to formally request my hand in marriage, and I got my first look at him. My heart in my mouth, I peered through a gap in the curtains from an upstairs room as he came to the door. What a relief. I saw the most attractive well-built young man, who looked extremely able. At the contract signing a week later, I suddenly became so shy I could barely raise my eyes from the floor."

Shades of Matilda's wedding, I thought, and asked, "And that was it?"

"No. There were six weeks before the wedding. During that time, he came to call often. He was so intelligent and charming that I think I fell in love with him very quickly. We talked about everything imaginable and agreed on so much that I felt I could really trust him."

"And then they got married and lived happily ever after," Elvira exclaimed.

"Yes, and no," Lucie countered. "Happy as a couple in love but much of the time hardly happily. I adored my husband; he adored me. We shared a life together as true partners, but as you shall see, a great deal of the time it was a life of terrible peril and misery."

She cut off suddenly. A family was approaching the church with the vicar to look it over for a wedding. But before she vanished, Lucie promised to tell me how she was introduced at court and how the true and terrifying aspects of the revolution finally got underway.

THREE

"*T*ell us about your wedding," Elvira said. "Was it very grand?"

"If you mean processions and trumpets and all that, no," Lucie replied. "But if you mean for the people who attended, it was indeed a very great affair that took place in a chapel."

It was excessively warm when I met them again, and a thunderstorm threatened. "We can stay outside until it rains," Elvira said.

"But what if I'm inside and the vicar should come back early?"

"You'll tell him you found the door open. He's very forgetful," Elvira said, then launched right in with her question about the wedding. Elvira was an incurable romantic and was insatiable in wanting to know anything and everything that had to do with love and marriage, both of which had been so sadly denied her during her all too brief life.

"There were all my mother's and father's relations and all of his, with nearly everyone a count or a countess. And of course, in honor to the two great families that were uniting, there were also all the Ministers of State, the Archbishop of Paris, and a small army of other prelates and titled people whose names escape me now."

"What did you wear?" I asked. Matilda's wedding, seven hundred years earlier, had prepared me for taking in stride such a high-level assemblage of people.

Lucie said, "I dressed quite simply for those days. I wore a gown of white crepe overlaid with fine Brussels lace and a bonnet. Veils weren't in vogue at weddings in my time. I had a cluster of orange blossoms in my hair and another pinned to my waist. The service lasted forever, and afterward we feasted at a table set for a hundred. There was another equally long table for peasants and workmen in their hall. When I visited them, they all rose and warmly toasted my health and future in a way that clearly told of their fondness for me, which meant far more to me than all the good wishes of the nobility."

"I bet your grandmother just loved that," Elvira said.

"Not half as much," Lucie said, "as when told two days later that the queen wished me to be presented to her only by Madame d'Henin. My grandmother could barely hide her fury at being cut out of the ceremony as well as being unable to continue to bully me, as I was now about to enter the queen's intimate court."

"Hurrah," cried Elvira, and I did likewise and clapped my hands, feeling this had just happened yesterday and not hundreds of years ago.

Elvira, who by now, I had learned, was scared of nothing, then asked the question I hadn't nerve enough to ask. "Lucie," she said suddenly, and all coy, which was totally unlike her, "There's something I want to ask you. What was it like? I mean, your wedding night."

Lucie burst out laughing. "You little devil, you. What was it like going to bed with a man for the first time?" She grew thoughtful. "All right. I was the luckiest girl alive because my brand new husband had fallen in love with me just the way I had with him, and he was the most wonderful lover that any woman could ever hope for. Throughout our entire marriage our intimate life was—well, it was just as perfect as two people who never stopped being in love could ever hope for."

Now it was Elvira's turn to laugh. She pointed a finger at me "Look, Alicia's blushing."

And I guess I was.

"Elvira, behave yourself," Lucie commanded sternly, and winked at me, which made me feel better. "Now, where was I?"

Relieved, I said hurriedly, "You were about to be presented to the queen."

"Ah, yes, and I'd just as soon not remember any of that," Lucie said. "I was beautifully gowned and decked out in more diamonds than you can imagine, including a whole necklace belonging to the queen herself, which she kindly lent me for the occasion.

"I made a fool of myself, however. I had to come up to the queen, who was seated on a wide throne with some ladies-in-waiting. Cloistered for years in the country, I was absolutely terrified. I managed to curtsey correctly three times the way the queen's dance master had spent hours showing me, and to remove a glove to lift and kiss the hem of her dress. But then I became completely tongue-tied, and when the queen beckoned me to sit beside her and began asking me questions, I felt the tears begin to flow. She was very kind, and told me not to worry, but I don't think she ever quite forgave me. She had little use for those who couldn't manage ceremony correctly.

"After I had been presented to the queen, I was presented to the king and his ducal brothers, with all their various equerry, and I knew that every male eye roving my body was imagining what my new husband took to bed. I sought refuge in the fact that I was probably far better educated than all of them put together. Worse was that evening at the ball. I was scrutinized the entire time by hundreds of critical eyes, and I knew that every word I spoke would be a principal topic of gossip the next day.

"The queen wanted me to wait two years for that while I became well settled in society. So basically my life became a relatively peaceful idyll of important social dinners and evenings at the theater in Paris as well as time spent in the country, and I did quite a bit of riding in the great forest of Compiègne on a perfectly lovely gray Arabian mare, which my archbishop Uncle had given me.

"There were dark spots, however. I lost my first child at birth. A little boy. It took me weeks to recover my spirits. Then there was trouble in Holland, where France had major political interests. My husband's regiment was put on alert, so I saw only half as much of him. Since neither he nor I had money to buy a home of our own, I was stuck at my grandmother's, and although she didn't dare attack me openly, as she had before my marriage, she nevertheless found ways to be as hurtful as ever."

"That's awfully sad about your child," I said. "I'm so sorry."

Elvira agreed, and then asked, "But what about the revolution?"

"It was brewing, no doubt of it," Lucie said, clearly glad to abandon a painful memory. The ruling class of French nobility, however, especially the king and Marie Antoinette, was dancing its way to the precipice, blissfully unaware of the misery and seething anger of the population in Paris.

"The winter of 1788 and 1789 was the worst in living memory. The French people were perilously close to famine. People died of the cold, and as I told you, the Duke of Orléans, the King's brother, began his evil subversion," Lucie said, "which gets me back to where I left off after the attack on Versailles and when the court had to move into the Tuileries Palace in Paris."

"Just a little country inn," Elvira said, and not without a touch of bitterness. It made me wonder how she must have felt, coming from a poor farm family, when hearing about lives, first from Matilda, then Sofo, and now Lucie, that were so far beyond her own. Elvira was mischievous in many ways, but so much of her few short years had been so awful that I felt she could be forgiven almost anything.

"Life seemed to go on as usual," Lucie continued, "except the genie had been let out of the bottle. The National Guard began to break up into units for and against the monarchy. The National Assembly forced the king to sign a constitution that virtually left him no real power, and finally he did the stupidest thing imaginable."

"Worse than firing the finance minister?"

"Far worse. He and the queen, with their children, tried to sneak out of Paris disguised as servants and with their servants disguised as nobility."

Elvira burst into peals of laughter. "From la-di-da riches to rags."

"And of course they were caught," I said. "What fools."

"Exactly," Lucie echoed. "The flight so enraged the Third Estate, now dominated by a group called the Jacobins, who were noted for their red hats and sashes, that they stripped the king of nearly all his remaining powers."

I sensed far worse was to come, and asked, "Then what?"

"The king then tried to regain his power by waging unsuccessful war against Austria, and that was a last straw. When the price of food shot up sky high, a mob attacked the Tuileries Palace and slaughtered the Swiss Guard. All two hundred of them. The king was arrested and imprisoned with the queen. That was in August of 1792. In September, the National Assembly voted to end the monarchy. France was proclaimed a republic, and the assembly assumed the new name of the National Convention, with a Committee of Public Safety as the executive."

"Where were you then?" I asked.

"I was at The Hague in Holland. My husband was sent there as French minister by the king when Louis was still in power. But with the National Convention now running France, my husband was recalled. It was a long cold trip back that I made alone with Marguerite and my second little child, Humbert. All the way we ran into unruly mobs of French soldiers who assailed me and Marguerite with the most vile obscenities and insults as hated 'aristos.' We were terrified, but even more frightened when we finally arrived and found Paris a city of fear.

"We stayed with my dear beloved father-in law, the Marquis de la Tour de Pin, who had been dismissed from his post as Minister of War. The king was tried for treason, and in 1793, on January 21st, the gates of Paris were closed and he was executed. Soon my father-in-law was also arrested and knew he was doomed."

I thought it all terrifying. Elvira shivered and said so.

"It was just beginning," Lucie said. "The National Convention then was taken over by the merciless

Jacobins, and under their leader, Maximillian Robespierre, the Terror began. My husband and I, urged by my father in law, left Paris. With troops and spies guarding every exit from France, it was impossible to leave the country, so we decided to go to the family estates outside Bordeaux, where there was still considerable loyalty to the monarchy. It was a move that would eventually grant us freedom, but only after an endless agony of fear. Even now it is hard for me to talk about it.

"My sadness at parting from my father-in-law, whom I knew I would never see again, nearly consumed me, and I only found partial relief in finally seeing his beautiful home, named Le Bouilh. Every corner of it spoke of his character and personality. For four months Frederick and I lived a quiet life of peace. I was several months' pregnant; it was April and the beginning of spring. We read endlessly, took quiet walks in the beautiful countryside. I made clothes for the baby and our little son. But that period was just the calm before the storm. The next time we meet, I shall tell you all about how we were forced to leave that lovely place and go into hiding."

"Oh, Lucie—now," I pleaded.

"Next time," Lucie said firmly.

There was reason for her breaking off. The old clock on the tower clanged the hour of six, and she knew that I had to be home to help with getting supper ready.

She left with a smile, and after she'd blown me a kiss, Elvira followed, and I was left alone in the quiet churchyard. The sun was still up, birds singing. High overhead I heard the drone of a passing aircraft. It all seemed so removed from angry mobs in Paris, solders gone amuck from lack of leadership, the horrible image of the king being led up the scaffold, the dreaded blade of the guillotine rattling downward to end his existence. Soon after him it had been the turn of Marie Antoinette. She went to the guillotine, and not in court dress covered with diamonds, her hair a tower of powder and perfume, but with a tattered shift only half covering her nakedness and with her hair hanging in knotted unwashed tangles around her bare shoulders. Gone was the most ornate of gold and silver carriages mastered by liveried coachmen. In its place she rode, shoeless and hands bound, in a wooden-wheeled peasant oxcart surrounded by a mob of jeering, laughing people hurling obscenities and filth at her.

I lay awake a long time that night, thinking of that poor woman and fearing Lucie would meet the same fate, even though I knew she had escaped it, and wondering how on earth she had. It brought me to comparing her always precarious life with my own. She'd lost children, and I'd I lost my mother and little brother. For a moment I was overwhelmed with the sadness of both. But what we shared stopped there. I could hardly compare Lucie's fleeing for her life from one home after another and, in America, to a semi-wilderness log house with no running water or heat to my leaving our lovely colonial in Connecticut for an equally comfortable rented home in England.

Biking back up the lane to dinner, I realized that listening to Lucie had made me feel less destroyed by my own loss of Mom and Tinker. In spite of everything, Lucie had kept going, and I remembered Mom always saying, when I was at rock bottom, "Get up and count your blessings." It made me think how lucky I'd been to have had Mom for as long as I had, and how lucky I was now to still have Dad and Arielle, and I felt better for it.

FOUR

To my relief, when we next met, Lucie dove right in where she'd left off.

"All the wonderful peace and quiet of Le Bouilh," she said, "and for once having my husband all to myself … all that finally came to an abrupt end."

"What happened?" Elvira demanded.

"What happened was that the horror of Paris, the Jacobin army of butchers, was on its way to Bordeaux dragging the dreaded guillotine behind it and with heads rolling all along the way. It was at once clear that we had to abandon Le Bouilh because surely it would be sequestered. All nobility or clerical personal property in France was being seized, and the Jacobins might well establish a garrison there. But where to find refuge? I was too far gone to be able to endure the long and dangerous flight to the Spanish border.

"The seemingly ideal solution came from a Monsieur de Brouquens, a friend of my father-in-law who lived in Bordeaux, where he was important in the city's administration. He had a small cottage named Canoles about ten miles from Bordeaux that was completely isolated in the middle of acres of vineyards. Reached only by various narrow farm roads that would allow us to escape by any of several routes, it was used only to house workers at harvest and for storing harvest records and representative wines, which were kept in the cellar. We had hardly settled in there in when two things happened. First, the guillotine arrived in Bordeaux and was set up permanently in the Place Dauphine, the large open square right in the center of town."

Lucie paused, and I felt shivers run up and down my spine.

Elvira piped up. "Was your baby arriving the second thing?"

"Yes," Lucie affirmed, "A little girl named Seraphine. My husband had found an excellent doctor to help, and for once I had no difficulty."

"Good," I exclaimed.

Lucie smiled wryly. "The good didn't last, unfortunately. It was only two days after Seraphine arrived that we received breathless word from a loyal servant woman of Monsieur de Brouquens that he had been arrested. He had been saved only because he was in charge of all the food supplies for the French army, which at the time was fighting in Spain. His Jacobin captors, however, insisted on his coming with them to Canoles to examine his harvest records, believing that he might have more there than that.

"It was quite clear that my husband had to flee for his life. We parted with neither of us having any idea if we'd see each other again or, for that matter, live another day. If the Jacobins were to learn my identity, I could have been on my way to the guillotine in a matter of hours."

"Where did your husband go?"

"He went first back to Le Bouilh, only to find that the Jacobins were nearly there. He had just time to saddle a good horse, and putting on peasant clothes, he fled for a second estate of his father some distance away, at Tesson, where the concierge and his wife were loyal to him."

"How long did he stay there?"

"He never got there. The weather was terrible, and during a storm he stopped at a small house for shelter where, unfortunately, a local mayor who also was staying was a Jacobin supporter. He demanded to see my husband's passport. My husband's wasn't good for the area he was in, and he only just got away before the mayor could have him arrested. He had to change course then. Dodging roadblocks and bands of Jacobin soldiers, he headed for a small town where one of his father's former grooms lived. This man didn't dare put him up, however, because of fear his small children might talk. He sent my husband on to another village to a man named Potier, a locksmith. He was loyal but as terrified as everyone was. One trace of loyalty to nobility and you were as good as

beheaded. He agreed to hide my husband, nevertheless, although for a substantial payment. Frederick was
put in a tiny windowless store room above the locksmith's forge. There he was stuck for three months,
without light or heat, and cautioned never to make
a sound that one of the apprentice locksmiths might
hear. He could only come out after work hours to get
some of the food that the locksmith's wife provided
with great care so it would not seem to neighborhood
shops that she was buying extra to feed someone."

"Meanwhile, what about you?"

"Well, I was at the mercy of the servant woman,
who fortunately was a very good person. I was on the
ground floor in a little room off the kitchen where
I'd given birth and had my three-day-old Seraphine
in bed with me. The terrified doctor hid in an alcove
in the room next to me, which the servant woman
barred from sight with a bed and my son Humbert's
cradle. Marguerite, who'd fled with us from Paris, had
come down with some sort of sickness and a high
fever, and I had sent her to one of two small rooms
upstairs in the cottage.

"We didn't have to wait long for the Jacobins. A
dozen of them, wearing the red Jacobin hat and sash,
soon arrived with dear Monsieur de Brouquens. The
good woman had set out food, and while the doctor
and I lay in a terror beyond description, scarcely daring to breathe, they quickly polished it off and drank
bottles of rare vintage wine like water. Eventually, one
of them demanded to know who was in the bedroom.
Monsieur de Brouquens, although as frightened as

we, again saved the day. He told them it was the young daughter of a friend who needed to have her out-of-wedlock baby in secret and who had given birth only a day before. A mild cry from Seraphine helped his story, and thank God they believed him."

I think both Elvira and I heaved a sigh of relief. "Did they stay long after that?"

"Only long enough to drink what remained of the wine."

"You must have been a wreck. What happened next?"

"There was an upside to their visit. Once they had cleared the place they were almost certainly not coming back soon, so what happened next was that the doctor and I came out of hiding. The good servant woman returned to Bordeaux with Monsieur de Brouquens, and my dear Marguerite recovered to take her place."

"Hurrah!" both Elvira and I exclaimed together.

"Yes, we could breathe again, but we couldn't leave Canoles. Nor could the poor doctor. Any place else was far too dangerous."

Again, Elvira and I both spoke at once. "How long did you stay there?" and "What happened to your husband?"

Lucie quickly answered both questions in order. "I stayed at Canoles almost six months," she said. "Meanwhile, my husband lived through some harrowing moments. The only reason he wasn't caught was the kindness and loyalty of those who had once served either him or his father. His refuge with the locksmith, Potier, unfortunately came to an end when one day in Bordeaux that good man saw a peasant like himself brought up on the scaffold, and he learned man died because he was caught sheltering a nobleman. He panicked. He came back to his forge and told my husband he would have to leave at once.

"This threw Frederick back into the hands of my father-in-law's groom. He buried my husband under a load of straw in an oxcart and took him to Frederick's lovely château at Tesson, which had not yet been seized by the Jacobins. On the way, one of the cutthroats at a Jacobin road block jabbed a pitchfork into the straw to make sure it didn't hide anyone. One prong of the fork stabbed my husband in the leg, but he managed not to move or cry out, and the cart was allowed to continue on.

"At Tesson, my husband found himself in the hands of Gregoire, the old concierge, who with his wife greeted him joyfully, doctored his leg, and hid him in a room in the servants' quarters next to theirs. He was then able to keep warm and rest a few days, marred only by his endless anxiety for my safety.

"But this only lasted eight days. The Jacobins finally came to seize the château. My husband fled again, this time with the help of Gregoire, to the home of a Monsieur Boucher, the postmaster in a nearby small village who had once also been a groom in my husband's grandfather's entourage and was a loyal royalist. Boucher had connections that would enable him to smuggle my husband south to areas that were in revolt against the new regime and being ignored by the Jacobins.

"But to the consternation of both my husband and the good Gregoire, Monsieur Boucher was away transporting goods to the French armies. His sister was willing to hide my husband, but this only lasted three days when she got word that her brother was returning, although not alone. He was being obliged to house some leading Jacobin officers and their staffs, and there would no longer be any room where she could hide Frederick."

"Oh, no," I cried. "What did he do?"

"Went back to Tesson."

"But what about the Jacobins?"

"Having seized the place and inventoried all its effects, they had left. Frederick was then stuck there for an addition two months. There was always the chance that some mistake Gregoire or his wife might make would reveal his presence, but there was no place else for him to hide. All the while, he was almost sick with anxiety and fear for me. Was I still at Canoles? Had I been arrested? What about the two children? He had no way of knowing."

"You couldn't get a message to him somehow?"

"I didn't know where he was or even if he was still alive."

It didn't take much imagination to picture how frantic both Lucie and her husband must have been. "That's so awful," I said. "What happened next? I mean, you said you were at this Canoles place six months. Then what?"

"*Then what* was this," Lucie replied. "I had begun to fear people would start asking why the young lady and her baby were staying there so long. So did the dear doctor. Rescue came via a young friend of Monsieur de Brouquens. His name was Chambeau, and he was to become a friend for many years. He rounded up another young man named Bonie who lived in a small apartment in Bordeaux and whose method of hiding himself was to do it in plain sight by wearing the Jacobins' rough trousers, their wooden shoes, their red bonnet and sash from which he hung a saber. He shouted their slogans, cursed aristocrats whenever and wherever he could, and glorified the revolution. Since he was not one of their officials, he was warmly regarded as a sympathizer. I moved into a small apartment in his house in a back street of Bordeaux."

"Wasn't that awfully close?" I asked.

"Too much so for comfort," Lucie replied. "It was only a few blocks from the guillotine at the Place Dauphin. Unless I stopped my ears, I constantly could hear the roll of drums and shouts of the crowd announcing that the deadly blade had just fallen. The sheer ghastly horror of it sickened me. Meanwhile I was too English-looking, which was all right for Paris and the court at Versailles but not for Bordeaux. Both English and American merchants were being packed off to prison, I don't know why, and questioned to make sure they weren't cheating the government. They even took people off merchant ships tied up at the docks. If that should happen to me, I would surely be discovered. Bonie immediately advised me to change my dress, and I covered my blond hair with a red scarf and wore the kind of ordinary clothes worn by Bordeaux shopkeepers' wives. That way, I was able to go out and visit Monsieur de Brouquens, who was still under house arrest."

"You actually went out?"

"Yes, and a number of times I had to walk through the Place Dauphine where the dreaded scaffold was, even, while it was in operation, requiring me to elbow and push my way through crowds. Knowing that one slip on my part would see me have an equal fate, it took every bit of self-control I could muster not to scream and run.

"Monsieur de Brouquens had finally learned through the grapevine of loyalists where my husband was, and that way I was able to get letters from Frederick. They would be delivered hidden in the center of a loaf of bread with no salutation and no address by a young boy who had no idea of what he was doing."

"How on earth did they manage that?"

"I never asked. While the Terror lasted, you learned to keep questions to yourself. To say nothing to anybody about anything. One false word, even the wrong facial expression, could mean the end of you. Every day I thought would be my last. What would happen to my poor innocent children, to my wonderful loving husband? I went to bed each night sick with fear and awoke filled with dread.

"Day and night, they were everywhere: in every tavern, every marketplace, on every street, in every house—looking for any aristocrat or noble they could seize. The Place Dauphine was awash with blood. They murdered four thousand in Bordeaux in just a few months. And there I was, right under their noses. The endless horror of it all finally began to make the good Monsieur Bonie nervous at my presence, and I knew he might soon be forced to ask me to leave. But where would I go? I couldn't see how I could possibly survive any longer, and I don't think I ever would have, nor my husband, except for a God-given stroke of luck that seemed too good to be true."

Lucie paused. I was too frightened by everything she told us to be able to speak and ask her what kind of luck. She collected her thoughts and continued. "Here's what happened. I ran into someone I had known well in Paris and for whom I had once done such a big favor that she'd always said she would be willing to do anything to repay me. She was a Madame Fontenay, a warm and lovely young person who had gotten herself rather lost and become the girlfriend of a man called Tallien. Although highborn, he had become an important person among the Jacobins.

"My first fear that she might disclose my presence in Bordeaux was soon put to rest. She greeted me with the affection of a sister and told me she would do anything possible to help me in my precarious situation."

"And did she?"

"Yes. And that 'anything possible' happened quite unexpectedly and very soon. She and I chanced to learn that an American ship, the *Diane,* was going to depart for Boston in eight days." Lucie paused, remembering, and then said, "You know, to everyone in life there always comes a moment when you have to roll the dice and pray. Without a passport, the ship's captain would never take me, and I didn't have one. Nor did my husband. I'd learned he was at Tesson, but how could I get word to him soon enough for him to join me? Worse—how could I get passports for either of us when I would have to apply for them to the Jacobin Governing Council? The mere sight of me would lead me to the scaffold. So it was with my heart in my mouth that I asked Madame Fontenay to intervene on my behalf with Monsieur Tallien."

"And did she?"

"Yes. She arranged a private meeting with him that very evening, which I will never forget. For a start, he terrified me by listing off all my relatives who'd been executed and by pointedly reminding me that I had been a lady-in-waiting to Marie Antoinette. He was a cat playing with a mouse. I was ill when he abruptly dismissed me and told me he'd consider my case.

"I don't know how I got back to Monsieur Bonie's house. I was sure I had made a mistake and that my children would be deprived of their mother and their only protection. All night, I lived in an agony of suspense, expecting at any moment to hear the dreaded knock on my door that would announce that the Jacobins had discovered my presence. The next day, the knock came, and instead of being led to the scaffold, I was greeted by none other than Madame

Fontenay and Monsieur Tallien together. This time the dreaded man was all smiles, and with the utmost courtesy—I'm sure to impress his mistress—told me he had issued an order to the Governing Council to provide a passport in the name of Latour for Frederick, me, and both our children. The stated purpose for it was to allow us to go to Martinique to arrange a sale of property that I owned there."

"It must have been incredibly scary," I said.

"Yes, but fear had become such a part of me that all I could think of was getting word to my husband to come out of hiding. While I racked my brains trying to think of some way, the wonderful Monsieur Bonie said that the only person to be trusted was himself, and right away he set off for Tesson. How, with his red bonnet and sash and saber, Bonie so terrified the good Gregoire into almost refusing to reveal my husband and how, with my husband dressed as a peasant, he commandeered a ride in a peasant cart all the way back to Bordeaux is a story in itself. It took them several days.

"On safely reaching Monsieur Bonie's home, my husband was hidden in a separate room so as not to arouse suspicion in the maidservant. I spent one night not knowing he was only a few yards away. After a joyful reunion the next afternoon, we summoned up our courage and presented ourselves as the Latour family before the Jacobin villains at the Governing Council, my husband mute and pretending to be hopelessly infirm and I, as an American woman, barely speaking a word of French.

"It was seven-thirty at night, and the council closed at eight. Several people were before us, one of them, poor devil, was summarily arrested right there, and nobody could doubt what his fate would be. When it came to us, the clerk told us to come back the next day, saying he'd done enough. You can imagine how our hearts sank. But Bonie once again saved the day. He offered to fill out the passport for the clerk if he was too tired to, and when that was done he caught some other official who was in such a hurry to rush out and dine that he signed the passports without even looking at them.

"Meantime I had arranged for passage on the *Diane* through an old friend of my father who was the Dutch consul in Bordeaux. To avoid the danger of our being in the same house together, my husband stayed with him in his little château near the Quai des Chartrons where the *Diane* was docked. There were still several days before it sailed, and I was able to pay a last tearful visit to my beloved Marguerite, who was staying with Monsieur de Brouquens. Also staying with him was the young Monsieur de Chambeau who had introduced the life-saving Bonie to me. The Jacobins had learned of his presence in Bordeaux, and he was obliged to flee for his life. But to where? I suggested, half in jest, that I should give him power of attorney to manage my affairs in Martinique. He leapt on that like a drowning man. It worked With the help of Monsieur de Brouquens, he was able to secure a passport and planned to board the *Diane* with us.

"The day of sailing finally came. I took little Humbert in tow and with Seraphine in my arms made my way down the Quai toward where the *Diane*'s captain awaited us. A dinghy manned by several sailors was to take us to the ship, which had moored across the estuary some distance away. It was a long walk to the dinghy. With every step I took, I was convinced I would hear the sudden shout of 'Stop' behind us and find myself arrested. But nothing did happen, and I found myself joined again by my husband in the dinghy, being rowed toward the *Diane*."

"Hurrah," I said, and Elvira joyfully cried out the same.

"Not yet," Lucie cautioned. "There was a slight fog, and out of it suddenly appeared a French warship that had anchored between us and the *Diane*. I think my heart stopped once again. The agonizing moment when they demanded to see our papers became unbearable when the captain was ordered to board with them. My husband and I were nearly paralyzed with fear, and I actually thought to throw myself overboard and drown to avoid the dreaded scaffold with its terrifying machine of death, until I felt little Humbert, who had sensed our terror, desperately clinging to me.

"Then, quite unexpectedly, we were saved. There was the sound of laughter and oars, and out of the fog came a long-boat filled with boisterous soldiers. For a moment we were forgotten in greetings between the soldiers and the warship's sailors. Our captain scrambled back into the dinghy, and we were rowed away as fast as possible.

"The *Diane* was small, nothing more than a coastal sloop. It had just one mast and, other than jibs, just one big sail. She was manned by only three sailors, a cabin boy, and the captain, who was quite young and turned at every moment for advice to an old man named Harper. Terror from the Jacobins or no, I think any one of us might have had second thoughts about leaving France if we had realized what we were in for. The trip took over six weeks."

I thought of my own seven-hour trip in a jet. "Six weeks? But that's terrible," I cried. "What happened? Why?"

"*Why* was that America was at war with Algeria. For that reason, the captain decided to steer north for fear of Algerian capture, which meant slavery. But to our consternation, he insisted on staying relatively close to the French coast, where the Algerians might not dare to sail. This put us in constant fear of the French, and our fears soon proved well founded. About ten days out of Bordeaux, a shot across our bow announced that we'd met up with a French frigate. We were ordered aboard, which the captain, thank heaven, refused to do because of the incredibly rough seas. We were bobbing up and down like a cork. The French commander then ordered us to follow him into Brest, the harbor in the northwest of France, calling for obedience with another shot that nearly struck us. Once again almost paralyzed with fear, we had no alternative but to obey. And once again, as though by a miracle, we were saved, this time by night and an oncoming fog. The moment the French could no longer see us, our Captain spun around and headed south in the opposite direction.

"The rest was just an endlessly long voyage of incredible misery. We had very, very little to eat. My husband took to bed, desperately seasick. I was still nursing Seraphine, and my milk, with all the stress and inadequate food, was beginning to dry up. The cook, who had his hands full trying to make meals on the most primitive of wood stoves, wasn't shy about enlisting me, and I am glad he did. He was an intelligent young fellow from a farm outside Boston, and while he and I worked together, I learned a great deal about what lay ahead for us. Although perilously short of everything, we scraped up nameless mixes from rotting potatoes and beans. Trying to stave off hunger with biscuits that were filled with crawling weevils was a fact of life, even though stomach-turning and causing our gums to bleed. Rough seas that heeled over the boat until I was sure we would founder, along with icy spray lashing the deck made cooking doubly hard. You had to hang onto cooking utensils to keep them from flying overboard while holding on yourself for dear life to avoid the same fate. My hair kept getting in the way, so in a fury one day I got a knife and hacked it off quite short, amusing the captain and the sailors but angering my husband.

"Like mine!" Elvira cried, and laughed.

"A mirror image of you," Lucie said. "The captain's southward course took us close to the Azores islands in the mid-Atlantic. Realizing his error when we met a British ship, which gave us a couple of sacks of slightly rotten potatoes, he headed northwest again. As the weather grew cooler, we ran into more dense fog. For ten we days saw absolutely nothing, and we began to run short of water and had no idea where we were. On the twelfth of May, 1794, we emerged slightly from the fog and the captain's dog, a little black terrier named Black, began barking furiously and racing back and forth on the deck. She'd smelled land. When the fog lifted completely we found ourselves just outside the great Boston harbor, being approached by a pilot boat."

"Wow!" I was finally able to say. "You made it."

"We made it," Lucie said. "We were finally in America and free."

Both Elvira and I, who had been so silent for so long, immediately began bombarding Lucie with questions. "Did you land right away? What was Boston like? Were you able to get some fresh food? What did your little boy say when he saw land?"

"Humbert was speechless," Lucie said. "So was I. Green grass, trees. No more howling wind and forever thinking that the next wave would sink us. Even my poor husband managed to get his way up onto deck and smile for the first time in weeks. He looked like a skeleton, he'd lost so much weight."

We started to ask more questions, but Lucie held up a hand. "No more today," she said. "Next time we meet, Alicia, I'll tell you all about how we became farmers."

FIVE

nd she did. It was on one of those wonderful summer evenings, unique to England, and I guess about nine o'clock, and
Lucie jumped right in.

"Now, where was I?" she said, as Elvira and I
settled down. "Ah, yes. America. Boston Harbor.
First of all," she continued, "I could talk for a month,
which I'm sure you wouldn't want me to do, trying to
describe how we felt being finally free. No more Jacobins. No more Terror. It was almost impossible for
any one of us to completely grasp that there was no
danger of being arrested and dragged up the scaffold
to a terrifying death. Overwhelming joy, an almost
physical feeling as though heavy chains had been
unwrapped from all around our bodies, struggled in
all of us against lingering fear. The captain immediately saw that we were well provisioned and fed, and

the fresh milk and bread seemed better than if he'd given us a mountain of gold. The ship's owner, who was a charming and wealthy man, arranged a small apartment for us with two rooms and a garden in the home of three spinster ladies. So the day after we entered the harbor, we said a warm good-bye to the crew and especially to Black, who had become as attached to us as we to her. We were rowed almost a mile to shore, thoroughly exhausted, and were fast asleep for the first time in America, when I was woken by a dog scratching and barking at the door."

"Black!" I cried.

"Right," Lucie said. "She'd been tied up when we left, but the moment night fell and she was untied, she jumped overboard to follow us."

"But you said you were a mile from shore."

"Exactly. And the poor thing swam it. And what's more, she found us. She was soaking wet, worn out, and hungry, but I soon took care of that with a towel and a plate of leftovers from our dinner."

"Hurrah! But what did the Captain say? Did you tell him?"

"Of course, but he said that clearly the dog now belonged to us, and that was that. Black stayed with us for the rest of her life."

"How long did you spend in Boston?" Elvira asked.

"About a month. We'd hardly arrived when we received letters from our aunt, Madame d'Henin. She had sent them to the ship owner, praying with crossed fingers that we would eventually arrive safely. She had also written to a very dear friend, a Mrs.

Church, who was the daughter of General Schuyler."

"Who was he?"

"General Schuyler? He was famous during your Revolutionary War for stopping the British under a General Burgoyne from marching south from Canada to reinforce Lord Cornwall, the British general who was close to defeating General Washington. Schuyler saved Washington and the Revolution by his victory over Burgoyne in a battle at Saratoga in upstate New York. Mrs. Church had written to her father, and we had hardly arrived when there were letters from the general, urging us to come see him where he lived in Albany. He'd heard that my husband wanted to farm and said there were plenty of acres of excellent soil available.

"So after a month in Boston, we departed for Albany with wonderful memories of all the open-hearted people we had met who had made us so welcome. That is, all except for a few French there, who were ardent supporters of the revolution in France and who stormed off the moment they realized we were nobility who had barely escaped the guillotine."

"How did you make the trip?" I asked. "And how long did it take?" I had visions of a vast forested wilderness replete with whooping, face-painted Indians, bears, and savage mountain lions.

"Several weeks," Lucie replied. "The roads through some already well-developed farm country were remarkably good, passing here and there by small but rapidly growing villages. We traveled in two open carriages, each drawn by two horses, and we stayed at a number of country inns just off the road, which were always announced by a mail box. While primitive, the inns were warm and comfortable, and the hospitality was always more than anyone could ask for. Nearly all had a picture of George Washington hanging up, and at meals everyone always toasted him. Your first president was loved by everyone.

"At Albany, we were greeted warmly by General Schuyler, who had a perfectly lovely mansion in the best location in the rapidly growing town, and he arranged for us to stay with a prosperous farmer named Burton some miles to the west.

"We insisted on being part of the Burton family. I helped Mrs. Burton with all the household duties that I'd always had servants do for me, and my husband worked as a farm laborer for Mr. Burton so he could learn all the American methods of farming, which were quite strange to him. Do you remember young Monsieur Chambeau, who escaped with us? He came with us to Albany. He felt he would need to learn a useful trade, so he apprenticed himself to a carpenter in the little nearby town of Troy."

All the time Lucie was speaking, I was mentally comparing her former life in court at Versailles with helping a farmer's wife in half-settled New York State, and her titled husband, whose hands had never touched pick or shovel, helping with every sort of farm work, including ditch-digging.

She must have read my mind because she said, "You're thinking all that was quite a comedown from my former life, I'm sure, but in a funny way it was more of a 'come up.' For me, it was—how can I put it?—It was as though I'd been reborn. I had suddenly discovered reality, and I embraced it eagerly. No more court dress and those hoops that would hardly let you through a door. And the corsets it took two maids to lace you into and that made your waist so tiny you could hardly breathe."

"Or your hair all powdered and stuck up with pins and pomade and piled a foot higher than your head," I said.

"Gone forever … well, for as long as I was in America, anyway, thank God. I was soon wearing what all the farm wives wore, a plain blue and black-striped woolen skirt and a plain black bodice. And don't forget, my hair was now almost as short as Elvira's. When working, I piled it up helter-skelter from my neck and fixed it with a comb. And when I needed to go to a neighbor to borrow something and had to cross quite a wide stream where there was no bridge, just a jam of big logs that were being floated down to a sawmill, I'd hike up the skirt and leap from one log to another. I was terrified, I admit, but fortunately they were so packed together that none of them rolled me over into the icy water where I could have been crushed by other logs."

I'd see pictures of lumberjacks doing the same dangerous thing and was too awed Lucie doing it.by that to speak. I heard Elvira ask, "How long did you live with the Burtons?"

"A few months, until we found a farm to buy a few miles away. It was on a low hill across the river from the Burtons and maybe half a mile downstream from them. We had a view of much of the surrounding countryside and were fairly close to where they planned to make a road from Albany to Schenectady, so we would not find ourselves too isolated. Some owner fifty years before us had cleared a hundred and fifty acres of forest, where he'd grown corn and wheat, and there was a large kitchen garden for growing vegetables and a pasture full of fruit trees."

"Cool. What was the house like?"

"Simple but solid, and all on one floor. There were four rooms, one larger than the others and with a fireplace. It had been built up on a solid stone wall more than five feet high. The space under it served as our cellar and my dairy. The walls of the house were solid rough-hewn planks, and we had them coated with plaster inside, which made the whole interior quite pretty. Don't forget Monsieur Chambeau. He had learned to be an excellent carpenter, and he managed many necessary improvements about the place.

"I was in our little yard chopping at a leg of mutton with a cleaver when I heard a voice behind me greeting me in French. To my astonishment, it was Monsieur Talleyrand."

"Who was he?"

"Charles Maurice de Talleyrand Perigord was the foreign minister of France under Louis XVI. By guile and brilliance, he managed to survive the Terror and the Jacobins. He was seen by many as the most brilliant Frenchman ever, while an equal number saw him as the most treacherous. He had always been kindness itself where I was concerned. He was visiting America, where he had met with General Washington, and he had come north with an introduction to General Schuyler. He brought the welcome news from France that the Jacobins were out and their leader, Robespierre, had been executed. The National Convention had voted in a new constitution with two houses of parliament, much like the Commons and House of Lords in England. France was now governed by a body knows as *Le Directoire*, a group of five men newly installed each year. It was as though you had five presidents instead of just one.

"That was good news. France could breathe again. But there was sadness for both me and my husband because the end of the Terror had come too late for both our fathers as well as other loved ones whose deaths had been … for what? To make a bunch of sadistic crazies happy. It was impossible not to remember the guillotine.

"Talleyrand had almost not recognized me. Besides my hair and farm dress, I was wearing moccasins I had bought from some Indians."

"There were still Indians there?" I was surprised. What with the towns all growing up, and farms sprouting up all over, and a highway being planned, I had thought they had long ago departed.

"Yes, but not many. They were the Onondagas, the last of the great Mohawk nation, which had all but disappeared. They lived mostly around Lake Champlain. I paid for the moccasins with a small jug of cream from our cow, which they loved, and I soon abandoned any fear of them. I found one or two older women who could speak a few words of English, and I became good enough friends with them that I was often asked to explain their needs to some of the other farmers." Lucie paused, and then said, "About this time, and to my utter consternation, I was forced to do something that made me feel really awful."

"What was that?"

She drew a deep breath. "Farming the place turned out to be too much for my husband alone. He needed help. We looked high and low for somebody to hire, but there was nobody, and it didn't look as though there ever would be. So we had to buy some slaves."

If I'd been surprised by there being Indians where she'd lived, I was horrified at her having slaves. Lucie a slave owner? It didn't add up.

She smiled wanly as the expression on my face fully revealed what I was thinking. "Please believe that both Frederick and I were deeply distressed. Back then, slaves were a normal way of life nearly everywhere, all over the world, especially among the Arab people in Africa and the Mideast and even among African people themselves. Frederick and I, however, belonged to a growing number of people in Europe and America who believed that slavery was all wrong. It was the right of everyone, unless a criminal, to dignity and respect, and above all, freedom. But where we were concerned, it was either be a slave owner, or give up any idea of farming. There simply was no other labor."

I pictured poor African Americans all chained

together, being auctioned off to a crowd of white plantation owners, and I managed to get over my shock enough to ask Lucie if she'd had to go to a "slave market."

"No, thank heaven," she said. "There was a law in New York State that allowed a slave to be resold to another master if he wanted to be. I was able to get hold first of Minck, a delightful man and a jack of all trades, and then Minck's father, Prime, a man noted for his intelligence and his considerable knowledge of agriculture, which we could certainly use. Prime persuaded us to buy a third person he knew, which we did. We found a man who had a wife from whom he'd been separated for some time by slavery. Badly needing help in the house and with my growing dairy business, I bought her too. Her name was Judith. She adored her husband, and their happiness to be reunited and have their own private room in the granary was heartwarming, to say the least. The expense in buying all four of my workers was repaid a thousand times in their gratitude, loyalty, and hard work."

I had an anxious question, however. I took a breath and asked it. "Lucie, what happened to them when you left America and went back to France?"

"I granted them their freedom, of course," Lucie said. "And when I did it was the happiest moment in my entire life."

"Theirs, too, I guess," I said. I felt a wave of relief.

"All four slaves," Lucie continued, "came into our lives just in time for us to prepare for winter, and when it came, it came with a sudden rush. One day it was autumn; the leaves had finally come down from the trees and the forests were bare. The next, there were ominous dark clouds with a howling northwest wind. The ponds and lakes all froze over in a day or so, and the river was soon two or three feet of solid ice. That made it safe enough for us to drive our winter sleighs over. And then the snow arrived. A foot or so of it overnight."

"You had sleighs?" I asked.

"Yes—big, low, boxy things with two rows of seats, painted up gaily in red and yellow and pulled by two horses. We'd pile in, cover ourselves with heavy blankets and furs, and off we'd go. Our American neighbors were very friendly and welcoming, and all winter we spent many a delightful evening dining and talking half the night. We had visits with General Schuyler too where we caught up on the latest news from France.

"Then spring came with the same rush winter had. One day the world was white with its deep blanket of snow and the air frigid. The next, the air was soft and caressing, and it seemed only days before the river was a raging torrent with fast-melting snow, and field and forest were gaily colored with wildflowers greeting the warming sun. We had eight cows by then, and I was infernally busy with the milking and separating the cream and making butter. Just the same, I was able to get out and ride on a wonderful little mare I picked up for almost nothing from another farmer. She was one of the best rides I ever had, and we went all over the countryside, which enabled me not only to exercise but to get away from household drudgery as well as the dairy, which, even with Judith's wonderful help, always occupied me for endless hours. At the same time I could see what other farmers were doing and get acquainted with some of them.

"While there, we also went to New York, which was a trip I'll never forget."

"But it must have taken forever," I said, thinking of the primitive state of the roads and the length of time it had taken Lucie and her husband to get from Boston to Albany. "And been awfully tiring to the children."

"I left Humbert and Seraphine with friends in Albany, and instead of the misery they would have felt traveling, they both had such a perfectly wonderful time. Neither felt much like returning to our home when we came to collect them."

"Good," I said. And then, "What were the inns like?"

"We didn't stay at any," Lucie replied. "We went by boat down the Hudson river."

"By sail?"

"By sail. And all the way. Boats were able to sail all the way up to Albany, which had become a sort of extended branch of the port in New York. Farm goods, mostly oats and wheat and corn from New York and faraway places like Ohio, were sent down-river to ships from Europe. Manufactured goods from factories in Connecticut or New Jersey or from Europe got back up to us settlers that way, too.

"The trip took twenty-six hours in a well-equipped

sloop. As for what we saw, it quite took my breath away, especially the narrow gap in the mountains at West Point, where the Revolutionary Army had stretched a huge chain across the river to prevent British ships from sailing up it. Farther down, there were some miles of magnificent cliffs they called the Palisades. We docked at a place called Canal Street, where we were reunited with Monsieur Talleyrand. He was in New York on business and came to meet us with Mr. Alexander Hamilton."

"You met Hamilton? Awesome."

"I did indeed, and he was so friendly and hospitable. And can you believe it, Alicia, he spoke French like a Frenchman and was most wonderfully read, far more so than most of the titled men I had known back in France. My husband had to go to Philadelphia for three days and got to meet General Washington and also Mr. Franklin, Mr. Jefferson, and others. I felt ever so badly not to be with him and have that very great privilege, but I'd been ill with some sort of fever before we left our farm and my husband thought it better I didn't travel, since the trip from New York to Philadelphia by stagecoach took several days."

"How long did you stay in New York, then?"

"Three weeks. New York was not the big city it is now. It was almost all on the island of Manhattan, which then was called New York Island, although there was a village and shipyards in Brooklyn. The center of the city was down around Wall Street, and the city limits were around Canal Street. Beyond that it was forest and farms. But it was a beehive of activity.

There were numerous churches, and both sides of the island were lined with docked ships.

"It was all wonderfully exciting, but a sudden rumor of an outbreak of yellow fever made us flee back up the Hudson River to home, where we found a bumper crop of grain being harvested and our fruit trees groaning with the weight of apples, pears, and cherries. Our country air revitalized me, and I got to work with a vengeance making and selling our dairy products. The whole harvest month was pure happiness until we quite unexpectedly got hit by tragedy."

Lucie paused, her face suddenly sad, and I was unable to refrain from bursting out with, "What happened? What happened?"

"My darling daughter Seraphine. One moment she was the healthiest of little girls, and the next ..." Lucie broke off, and I didn't dare say the word that I knew was on her lips. She took a breath and said, "The doctors had no idea what it was that killed her."

I couldn't find anything to say at this awful turn of events. And I knew Elvira couldn't either. Both of us remained silent. I thought of Matilda and the children she had lost. And I thought of how lucky we moderns are to have access to life-saving medicine.

Lucie seemed to pull herself together and smiled slightly. "Well, death is something everyone has to get used to, isn't it? Although it's hardly easy. Our own lives couldn't stop. There was work to be done to prepare for winter, which came early that year and with a terrible ferocity. We found a way to mill and press apples and jug the juice to ferment into cider, which we sold at a good price. And, of course, there was all the usual storing of potatoes and yams and squash in a root cellar, our vegetables for the winter—there were no refrigerators then, needless to say. There were also all the other preparations for winter: getting our sleighs ready, checking on any harness repairs, and making any last-minute improvements to our buildings that would help strengthen them against the wintery blasts and plummeting temperatures we had learned would come.

"The winter was uneventful, except I had a bout of measles, which I was terrified Humbert would get, but he didn't, thank God. Then, just as spring was starting, and the cold winds turned south and were gentle and mild, and we saw the first V-shaped formations of geese flying high overhead, we got the news from France that required us to leave our American home."

"Oh, dear. Why? What happened in France?"

"Under the new constitution, *Le Directoire,* which had replaced the dreaded Jacobins, had ordered restoration of all private property that had been seized and did not belong to *émigrés.*"

"Which meant you and your husband could get back your estates?"

"Yes and no. We were told Frederick's mother had already regained family property at Tesson and several lesser properties. But there was a legal hitch of some kind where Le Bouilh was concerned, and it could not be returned to us except personally, and that within a year."

"It couldn't be returned to your husband's mother or someone who represented you?"

"No. And with news and mail so slow back in those days, several months had already gone by. There was no question of remaining in America any longer than absolutely necessary. It meant a huge inheritance to our little Humbert and any subsequent children. Only fools throw away fortunes. My husband was cautiously thrilled, of course."

"And you?"

"You know the answer. I was devastated. I was no longer the frivolous little lady-in-waiting to the queen, an immature spoiled noblewoman who had thrived on the obscene frivolity of the French royal court. I had been made a completely different person by four years of the Terror in which nearly every single minute of every day I feared would be my last, by the horror of what I had seen wrought by the guillotine, by endless sickening anxiety for my loved ones until our flight to safety in America, but even then with all the additional anxiety of settling in a foreign land we knew nothing of. Finally there was the reality of down-to-earth subsistence farming and the truth we saw through our slaves that all people, unless criminals, deserve respect and a peaceful life.

"The thought of leaving our little farm I had grown to love so, of abandoning the hard work and simple way of life that had become everything to me, broke my heart. The two years I spent in America were by far the happiest in my life. The day I left was the end of my life because the rest of my years on earth, which turned out not to be easy, was only living because one has to; because, if nothing else, it' is our duty to those who love us and are dependent on us.

"There was one bright moment in the wrenching misery of saying good-bye to friends and neighbors. It was when we granted freedom to our four slaves. Their happiness at finding themselves no longer 'owned' was almost impossible to describe. It helped lift some of our own pain. My husband was generous in giving them money to get restarted in life, and I hope that my very real tears and the warmth of my embraces helped them realize how much we had cared and wished for them.

"So that was it. We packed up. I knelt and prayed at the grave of my little Seraphine, who would now rest alone thousands of miles from us. Then, and with me feeling a strange presentiment that all was not going to turn out as optimistically as my husband felt, we went back to New York by boat and immediately booked passage.

"This time we sailed on a large four-hundred-ton English frigate with a crew of fifty, in luxurious cabins, and were served good food."

"Where did you land?"

"In Cadiz."

"But that's Spain," I said. "Why not in France?"

"Because at a frontier between France and Spain we would have a better chance of appraising exactly how stable or unstable the current government of

France actually was, and perhaps be able to avoid walking into a trap of some sort."

"And if things went wrong, you'd be able to return to America?"

Lucy smiled wryly. "I personally hoped so. My fondest wish was that some magic would instantly find me again on my farm, where I had enjoyed so much hope and peace, and where my darling daughter was laid to rest. But it wasn't to be. *Le Directoire* hadn't changed its mind, and we were indeed going to be able to regain our property, although I kept having a nagging presentiment that all was not going to turn out well.

"Landing in Cadiz was unfortunate, however. There were no boats that would take us up the Spanish coast to Bordeaux, nor any that would bring us east to Barcelona on the Mediterranean and virtually at the French border. Time was now running out, and we could no longer tarry, so we took the long route across Spain itself by wagon and on roads haunted by desperate, half-starved former Spanish soldiers who had been released from service the year before, when the war between France and Spain ended.

"It was an awful trip that took weeks. Sleep was nearly impossible from the heat, and I was again pregnant, and by the time we reached the frontier, heavily so. There, and to our delight, we were met by Monsieur Bonie, who had done so much for us in making possible our escape from the *Terror* two years before."

Lucie started to say something else but in the next second she was gone, and Elvira with her, and

I was alone in the churchyard, except for the vicar, who appeared with his elderly sister and two equally ancient friends.

SIX

Lucie said, "Now, where were we before the vicar and his bevy of dear old things interrupted? Ah, yes. My presentiment that we would encounter difficulties, being pregnant again and being met by dear Monsieur Bonie."

It was a bright, cheerful morning, and we were seated on the grass in the churchyard.

"Well," she went on, "my presentiment wasn't unfounded. Before we were allowed to go to Le Bouilh, Frederick was forced to endure hours of hostile questioning by the local officials all the way as to why he was back in France; what his political loyalties and his plans were. In Bordeaux we were greeted by our old friend and benefactor, Monsieur de Brouquens, and warned that even though the revolution was over, there were still Jacobins remaining in the government.

"Finally, I'm sure you can imagine, my shock when we reached Le Bouilh itself and found that wonderful château that I had loved so much had been stripped absolutely bare of all furnishings, and the kitchen pillaged by the Jacobins. Fortunately, a lot of the local people felt guilty at having bought much of our Le Bouilh belongings for almost nothing from the greedy Jacobins, and they returned them to us for what they had paid. So we got back a great number of things, and most importantly the large and valuable library.

"Sad as it all was, I had one wonderful burst of happiness when my dearly loved Marguerite showed up, hale and hearty from Paris, where she'd been hiding, as they had guillotined aristocrats' servants by the thousands, from head butlers down to the lowest scullery maid. She arrived just in time to assist in the birth of little Charlotte, my fourth child, and you can imagine the hours we spent telling each other all that had occurred to us during our separation.

"But in spite of my joy over Charlotte and Marguerite," Lucie continued, "It was a bitter winter. More and more every day, I yearned for America and my life there. Nights were the worst. Bands of brigands roamed the countryside, entering homes at night to rape and plunder. Sometimes, when my husband was away, I'd sit almost to dawn with two loaded pistols listening for the warning bark of Black and our other dogs.

"When spring came, my husband had to go to Paris to settle many of the family affairs. Again having a presentiment that things might turn out badly, I decided to go with him. There's a French expression, *Plus que ça change, plus c'est la même chose,* meaning the more things change, the more they stay the same. The Directory now suddenly allowed *émigrés* to return, and royalists who had fled were soon back in their old ways. I was the rage for a while, a real oddity because of my experience in America. Everyone seemed to think the life Frederick and I had lived was a sort of playtime for us—you know, dress up and play farmer. And then the roof fell in."

Both Elvira and I immediately cried out, "What happened? Now what?"

"Afraid of a royalist coup d'état, the Jacobins remaining in the National Council got the Directory to rescind its order allowing the return of *émigrés,* those who had fled the country. Hundreds were given only twenty-four hours to leave again or face imprisonment, including and especially Frederick and me, largely because of me. I was seen as a particularly loathsome and special person because I had been a lady-in-waiting to the hated Marie Antoinette.

"But that's crazy."

"It certainly was, and almost before I could think, I found myself in a carriage on my way to Calais on the Channel coast with my husband and children and the few things I'd taken to Paris from Le Bouilh."

"Why Calais? That would mean going to England. Wasn't that your chance to get back to America?"

"Because there was hope that the order would only be temporary and we'd be back quickly for my husband to finish all the business of regaining his estates for our children. That, after all, is why we'd left America. But as I feared, that hope turned out to be in vain. The order wasn't rescinded for two long years that I'd just as soon never remember. We were penniless, as my husband had not had the time to settle affairs that would have returned at least some of his money. Fortunately, through my father's family, we had English relatives and lived mostly on their charity. Both my grandmother and my archbishop uncle were also in England. She died, unlamented, soon after we arrived, and any hope of an inheritance from her was dashed as she left only debts. Then, as if that weren't enough, we were once again struck with personal tragedy. A lovely healthy little boy I produced and whom we named Edward died quite suddenly from pleurisy when only three months old."

"Oh, dear. I'm sorry," Elvira muttered. I said nothing. I couldn't. I stared at Lucie, and all I could think was that when this child died, she'd been about the age she appeared to me now, like some American girl in college. Everything she'd told me about, all the horrors of the revolution and fleeing the guillotine to America, where she lost little Seraphine, whom she loved so much, and then being forced to come back—all that had happened when she was only a year or so older than my sister, Arielle. How could any life be so full of so much? How could anyone suffer all that and still keep going?

Lucie's exile sounded awful, and I could see it was hard for her to talk about, so I asked her what happened when they were finally allowed back.

She immediately seemed relieved and brightened little. "What happened was one of history's biggest events. And it involved one of history's greatest men—someone who to this day is revered in France. Can you guess who that was?"

I put two and two together, and took a shot at it. "Napoleon?"

Lucie clapped her hands. "None other. He had finally evaded a British blockade, which had kept him and his army in Egypt, and had returned to France. In a coup d'état, he had installed himself with two others in a Consulate to replace the Directory."

"More people guillotined?" asked Elvira, with a definite hint of facetiousness.

Lucie took her seriously. "No, no. That was over forever. The coup d'état was bloodless, and we were safe to go home, although since England and France were at war, we had to go via first Holland and then Germany, and with Danish passports. A friend had rented us a charming small house in Paris, and we'd hardly arrived when I gave birth to a little girl we named Cécile. I'd hardly rested a few days when I then found myself in demand by Madame Bonaparte. This was Josephine, Napoleon's first wife. She had already installed herself in the Tuileries and had been instructed by him to develop a social circle of the leading members of the nobility whose highly important connections he would be able to use. She quickly saw me as the key to all of them, and hence I was obliged to see her quite often."

"So back to the unwanted job of being a social leader."

"Along with corsets and hairdos and fancy clothes," Elvira said.

"Don't tell me," Lucie laughed. "But at least the ridiculous *panier* hoops and hair being piled up into towers were gone. We wore it far shorter and often straight down, and our dresses were far simpler."

"What was she like?"

"I liked her. She was very warm and kind and not stupid. Almost overnight she had recreated herself from being just the wife of a soldier to being every inch a queen."

"What about him? I mean, he was a ruthless dictator, wasn't he? Like Hitler or Stalin?"

"Napoleon? Good heavens, no. He was far from it. And don't ever say that in France, where his memory is revered. All that thinking comes mostly from the highly prejudiced English, who only tell you about his conquests. They don't tell you that he was a brilliant civil engineer, and that half the roads and most of the canal systems in use in France today were planned by him. They don't tell you, either, that behind all his conquests was a burning desire to unify all of Europe into one nation much the way you are in the United States, or people are today in the European Union. He was two hundred years ahead of his time."

"He was still just a pudgy sourpuss," Elvira said, "seated on a big white horse with one hand shoved into his waistcoat and wearing a cocked hat."

Lucie burst out laughing, and said to me, "See

what I mean by English prejudice?" And to Elvira, "That was just one painting. Actually, during most of his life, he was lean and muscular, and had an incredibly magnetic personality. Women swooned when in his presence, and men laid down their lives for him."

"Did you ever get to meet him?" I was thrilled at being able to talk to someone who had talked to Napoleon. He hadn't lived that long ago, and it made me feel closer to Lucie than ever.

"I most certainly did," she replied, "but not for quite a while, because we soon went back to Le Bouilh, where we stayed for the next eight years."

"I'd hoped you were going to say America," I ventured.

"I know you were, but it wasn't possible, and Le Bouilh was the next best thing. I loved the place, and our years there were peaceful and happy ones. My husband went back to farming his vineyard, and I renewed many old acquaintances and raised our children, although early in our stay another terrible sadness struck me. My darling Marguerite took desperately ill, lingered for a week, and died. It took me months to face the fact that she was gone, and gone forever. Eventually I was helped out of my deep grief by the happiness of having another child, this time a little boy we named Aymar." She paused, remembering, then said "Meanwhile, the emperor had decided to divorce his wife, Josephine, in favor of Marie Louise, the daughter of the King of Austria."

"Oh, no," I cried. "Politics, right?"

"Right," Lucie replied. "Poor Josephine was

devastated, but at least she had the comfort of knowing it wasn't because of her or anything she'd done."

"You mean hadn't done," Elvira offered. "She hadn't had any children."

"Unfortunately true, and Napoleon was desperate for an heir, preferably a son, which would have strengthened the dynasty he was anxious to establish. He was also anxious to avoid further war with Austria, and the marriage would have gone a long way to fulfilling that wish.

"I then suddenly found myself on the move again. Napoleon appointed my husband prefect of Brussels, in Belgium, which at the time was French and an extremely important city. Being prefect was a big job and a great honor. But we soon had trouble. Everyone has enemies, and Frederick was no exception. Falsehoods and lies about him caused the emperor to recall him. Napoleon hadn't counted on me, however. My half-sister, Fanny, had come back from the Caribbean with my father, and she became engaged to Field Marshall Bertrand, Napoleon's top general. Because of all the necessary arrangements for the wedding, I was put in direct contact with Napoleon himself and saw a good deal of him.

"I took advantage of that, and it wasn't long before I found the chance to set things straight. In a private audience with him, I threw all caution to the wind to plead my husband's case. I think that at one point I so lost my head that I actually had the audacity to berate the emperor for his error. When I finally wound down and apologized for my passion, I will never forget what he said. 'Madame, I was wrong, but what can be done about it?' It was perhaps the only time in his life he admitted a mistake. Even better was what he said when I told him I was sure he could set things straight. He thought a moment and then said, 'I am assigning prefectures in France tonight. One of them is Amiens. Would that suit you?'

"I left Paris floating on air. Amiens was a real prize. It was far more prestigious than Brussels. Its prefecture covered a whole huge northern section of France. But regrettably, it was the last time I ever saw that great man."

"Why?"

"*Why* is history. He had mistakenly decided to attack Russia. Its huge well-generaled army slowly retreated, destroying everything—crops and livestock—that Napoleon's troops depended on. Then, when thousands of miles into Russia, the terrible Russian winter arrived, and with his army seriously weakened, he was forced to retreat back to France in his first great defeat. Under the Treaty of Fontainebleau, he was allowed to retire to the Mediterranean island of Elba, where he hoped to establish a world cultural center."

I vaguely remembered something of history, and I said, "Elba didn't last long, though, did it?"

"No, it didn't. The Bourbons, who were Louis XVI loyalists, had hardly rushed back in and got more or less established when Napoleon was back, virtually driven out of Elba by the allies Austria, France, and

Russia betraying the treaty. Half the country immediately rallied behind him. For a hundred days France again had an emperor until all was lost forever when Napoleon faced final defeat by Wellington and the English at the battle of Waterloo."

"What happened to you when he was on Elba? Were you then in trouble with the royalists when they came back?"

"Not at all. There was a new king, the guillotined Louis XVI's younger brother, and I found myself in greater demand than ever. As almost the last survivor of the Versailles court, I represented the grandeur that had once been."

"So after all that revolution and Terror, France was right back to being a monarchy?"

"Yes and no. They had a king, but it was a constitutional monarchy, pretty much like England is today. And that, dear children," she added, putting an arm around Elvira, "is the end of my story."

It was so sudden and so unexpected that I could hardly find my voice. "Oh, no!" I cried. "You lived years longer after that. I read you died in Italy at Pisa where there's that famous leaning tower."

Lucie's response was a kindly smile. Then her expression grew somber. "Children, no life is perfect. There are ups and downs, as you have seen from what I have told you of mine. So I would like to stop when everything was pretty much 'up.' My husband had reached the highest pinnacle of service to his country, he was First Minister to Vienna and then one of our ambassadors to the Congress of Vienna, the assembly of the principal powers of Europe to try to redefine borders so as to prevent more wars. My son, Humbert, was well on his way up the ranks of important civil service that would lead, among other things, to military distinction, and my daughter Charlotte had made a dazzling marriage to a man she adored and had given me a grandchild. My darling Cécile would soon travel the same route. I was revered wherever I went and was a very proud and happy woman."

"Except," I said, "you missed America still and making the best butter in the state of New York and being friendly with the Indians and freeing slaves."

"All that, yes." Lucie admitted. "I clung to that memory for the rest of my days. And still do in eternity. Whenever I felt down or things went badly for me or my husband, I thought of the farm, our wonderful neighbors like General Schuyler, myself leaping from log to log on the rushing river to get to the other side, the tremendous winters, the glorious springs and summers. My life on that little farm is one reason I've so loved talking to you, Alicia. Telling you about it has brought it all back to me so very vividly. Bless you for that."

She gave me a radiant smile, and then, before I could say a word, she was gone.

I think I must have been staring at Elvira blankly for a long time, my mind still back in Lucie's farm, because she had to say my name twice before I came to my senses and realized where I actually was.

"I'm glad she didn't tell you the rest of her life," she said. "It was something I know she tries not to think of, and it would have brought back too many sad memories."

"But what happened?" I said.

"Well as she told you, life has its ups and its downs. The rest of Lucie's life was a down, I'm afraid."

"But like what?" I insisted.

"Well, if you really want to know, but I'll keep it short." Elvira thought a moment, and then she said, "From all the chatter I've heard over the centuries, most revolutions don't just come and go in a few days. They hang around for quite a while. After Napoleon, the French went right on for another thirty years, kicking out kings and putting in new ones. First ..."

"Stop! "I cried. I can read all about the endless French revolutions in a book. I want to know what happened to Lucie."

Elvira bit her lip, clearly reluctant. "All right," she said. She held up one hand and began eliminating fingers, one by one. "First Charlotte's baby died, then Humbert got killed in a duel over some silly matter, then Cécile died of some unknown sickness, and then Charlotte died. Finally, if that wasn't enough, her son Aymar sided with plotters to throw out King Louis Philippe and was convicted of treason and sentenced to death."

I could hardly believe what I had heard. And now her son had been guillotined? "Aymar?" I cried.

"He escaped from France," Elvira said quickly. "But Lucie's husband was tossed in prison for three months for publicly defending him, and Lucie joined him to share the burden of it."

"She went to prison too?"

"Yes. Voluntarily."

I thought, that sounded like Lucie, all right. "And then what?"

"They both went into exile to be with their son. After some years, Frederick then died in Switzerland, and Lucie spent the remainder of her life, until she was eighty-three, in Italy, accompanied by Aymar, her last remaining child."

Poor Lucie, I thought. But as she would have said herself, I knew, that was life. You could never have everything perfect all the way. And I had to wonder: did she realize, even now, how extraordinarily successful in a way her life had been, the inspiring legacy she left for so many others of hope and determination and courage? I could grieve for Lucy, yes, and I certainly did, but I could also feel real happiness for everything she had been, for how she had lived the great gift of life to its fullest extent, not just for herself but always for others, too.

I planned, of course, to keep right on seeing Elvira, but plans in life often come badly unstuck. At dinner, Dad announced that his research at the British Library had ended. The rest of his work would be at Oxford, and we would be moving that very week to a university residential house arranged for us by his professor friend.

I was devastated. It meant no more visits to Elvira, at least not for any time in the predictable future.

Taking a page from Lucie's book, I won't go into how "down" our final parting was for me. I cried a lot, even though Elvira kept insisting over and over that one day I would be independent and I could come back to the valley on my own and visit Matilda's old Norman church and her again.

We went to Oxford. Then Dad decided to stay in England, "make a whole fresh start," he said. I went back to school there, an English one this time, and then ended up "reading" history at the university, helped in my application for admittance by Dad's professor friend as well as by papers I wrote on medieval and Renaissance societies and the French aristocracy during the revolution and the Terror.

Time sometimes erases so much. As days, then months, then busy years slipped by, and my entire being was concentrated on my studies—and to my surprise, a burgeoning social life—the pain of separating from Elvira lessened. I slowly began to think less and less about her. The old Norman church and everything I had experienced in its churchyard became only the dimmest of memories until I began to doubt I ever had actually seen and talked to her at all. Had Elvira just been fantasy? Had I actually met Matilda and Sofonisba and Lucie? Or had I simply either dreamed of them or imagined the meetings out of loneliness and the trauma of losing my mother? Dr. Resus, the therapist I'd had to see after Mon was gone, always said I was escaping so much into a world of history that I was in danger of substituting fantasy for reality. Had I actually done just that? The question left me with a strange sense of nagging guilt. At times, for no apparent reason, I'd feel an overwhelming sadness, almost the way I'd felt when we lost Mom and my little brother.

Then one day, when I chanced to be headed for London with Arielle, who had returned to America to live and was visiting, her presence provoked memories.

Reminiscing with her about our time together in the big yellow Thames Valley house revived my strange feelings of unease.

Dad and I are members of the National Trust, an organization dedicated to preserving historic homes and monuments. One such on our route was an old Elizabethan manor house, along with its granary and barn. It had been reconstructed to show how people lived back then, and I got a shock when we decided to stop and have a look. The entrance was marked by two ancient stone columns. On one there was a brass plaque that read THE 16TH-CENTURY FARM OF THOMAS BROWN.

Memories rushed in on me, vividly clear. Elvira saying her father's farm had two proud gateposts. And that her father's name was Thomas. It was as though Elvira was suddenly there with me and saying, "Hey, Alicia, what's with you?"

Bewildering Arielle, I headed right down the Thames Valley for Henley. Branching off the main London road to the Old Plough Horse pub, I told her to wait, and, leaving her even more puzzled, I set out on the tow path for the old Norman church. The moment I was out of sight I began to run, for all I was worth, and in a few utterly breathless minutes found myself at the churchyard. It was a beautiful summer day, just like the first day I had ever walked through the rickety old gate in the mossy old brick wall. Nothing had changed. There was even another little squirrel hopping about, larks sang above field and meadow, the air was perfumed and sweet, and high overhead I heard the whisper of an aircraft.

And there it was, Elvira's grave, its stone still as erect as when old Henry and I had put it back in place. I picked some wildflowers from against the brick wall and put them at the foot of her gravestone and knelt before it.

"Elvira? Elvira, it's me Alicia."

My heart pounding wildly, I waited. And suddenly heard that old familiar musical laughter, and Elvira herself was there, standing behind her gravestone, leaning over it, her corn-colored hair as chopped up as always, her eyes blue, blue like the sky, and admonishing mischievousness written all over her.

"Well, Alicia, you certainly took your time."

When later I got back to an anxious Ariella, she noticed at once that I had been crying, and put a comforting arm around me. "What's happened? Are you okay?"

"Never been better."

"But why the tears? Where were you? What were you doing?"

I didn't tell her. Not where I'd been and what I'd been doing and why, nor that my tears were from overwhelming relief and happiness. Elvira and my ghostly meetings and talks weren't fantasy trips. They were real. As real as my student life at Oxford, and as real as the lovely old Norman church surrounded by the weatherworn graves of so many lying there in peace. The ghosts I'd met and whose lives I'd shared were a reality I would love and enjoy for the rest of my life—perhaps even afterward. They were my very own special secret I would never share with anyone.

End

ABOUT THE AUTHOR

Born to wealth and privilege in New York, David Osborn chose to spurn both as false icons after World War II combat as a Marine Corps dive bomber pilot. On his own and following brief careers in television and public relations, he expatriated to France when falsely accused of un-Americanism in the infamous Senator McCarthy era, paying his way with a co-authored first motion picture script, *Chase a Crooked Shadow*. When its star-studded success took him from laboring in a rock quarry in France into Britain's film industry, he was launched on a long world-class writing career that saw him dangerously engaged during several Cold War years

with Czech anticommunist resistance behind the
Iron Curtain. Living in France and England as well
as isolated for twelve years in a tiny Alpine village in
Switzerland, Osborn authored numerous stellar TV
plays and a score of major motion pictures, including
The Trap, which earned an Academy Award nomi-
nation. Turning novelist with the critical success of
The Glass Tower followed by the world best-selling
classics *Open Season*, *The French Decision*, *Love and
Treason*, and a half dozen more outstanding thrill-
ers, he has had many imitators, but none reaching
the startling originality of his stories, the stunning
impact of his flawless page-turning plots, and his lit-
erate prose in each that packs a powerful punch with
nearly every line.